Evelyn

Noah Lust

Contents

Chapter 1 - Rose Colored Glasses

Chapter Song: Break My Stride by Matthew Wilder

EvelynI've found that the best way to face the world with some semblance of joy and a will to live is to look at everything through rose colored glass.

What started as a chore seems so natural to me now. I just changed my perspective. Now I notice how pretty the trees look after it rains. I see how kids eyes light up when they see something that astounds them. I see couples in love, a family of ducks crossing the street, Harry Styles releasing a new song, etc.

It's funny how a little change in perspective can change so much.

Some days I don't have to pretend I'm happy. I just am. It's refreshing.

Even now at work, I'm not focusing on the fact that I'm a miserable slave to the corporate mediocrity.

I'm taking a moment to be glad that I'm not working in Florida.

Anywhere in Florida.

Then again, nobody in their right mind works as a barista in California. Working customer service is signing your own death certificate with the cause of death written as harassment and verbal abuse.

But, hey, at least I'm getting paid.

Even for as rude as people can be, some are nice. There's a sweet elderly woman, Eleanor, who comes into the café every day at 8 o'clock and orders two muffins; one for herself and one for her granddaughter, who she drives to day care every day.

Sometimes I can't help but imagine myself as the little girl. Having a loving family to support and care for her no matter wh-

"Evelyn! The hell are you doing?"

I could recognize the earsplitting voice of my boss anywhere.

"I'm restocking the coffee cups," I reply simply.

"Who told you to do that?"

"You did."

My boss, Leah, didn't say anything as she turned around and marched back into her office.

Okay. That was fine.

It could've been worse. She could've fired me like she did Vanessa.

I turned back around to continue what I was doing when I knocked down the cups.

This is fine.

At least a customer isn't standing behind the counter to witness this.

"I'm supposed to be receiving some good customer service here, but so far all I see is an idiot."

Wow, someone poured salt instead of sugar into their coffee this morning.

"Sorry for the delay, how can I help you?" I asked the prissy girl behind the counter once I was brave enough to face her with a smile. She stared at me like I was the most disgusting thing she'd ever seen.

"Actually, nothing anymore. This isn't worth my time."

And. She. Walked. Out.

Good riddance.

~~~

I was about to clock out and go on my lunch, but then the doorbell rang.

And not to objectify, because I don't like or want to be objectified and I certainly won't do it to other people, but the most attractive guy I've ever seen in my life walked in.

He had dark brown hair and assessing green eyes. He wasn't smiling, in fact he looked kind of sad, but I bet he had a pretty smile. He was tall, 6'0 maybe? He looked like maybe he was in his late teenage years, early twenties.

But I don't know. I'm literally can't guess someone's age right to save my life.

Oh God, he's walking up to me.

Of course he is. He's a customer here. And I work customer service. All I have to do is take his order and not get flustered.
~~~

"Hi, welcome! How can I-" I started as I walked over to him before I tripped on one of the cups. Idiot. "How can I help you?"

"I'll have a chocolate muffin."

Wow, he has a pretty voice. It's quiet and deep but not deep like those posers who deepen their voice on purpose to try and impress girls but in reality they sound like they swallowed a bucket of asphalt.

"Okay," I said, my voice an octave or two too high.

I grabbed his muffin and tried my best to regain any of my remaining composure and dignity. He's just a guy, I talk to guys all the time. I could do this.

Then I saw my reflection in the glass. Today definitely wasn't doing me any favors. I was up late scrolling on TikTok for hours last night even though I knew I'd regret it later. But makeup and coffee seemed to hide that pretty well.

I had my hair tied back in a loose braid, but it might have been too loose. Small, dark strands started to unravel themselves from the braid and if Leah saw that I think she would kill me herself.

Unless I die of embarrassment first.

I walked to the cash register and he followed me along the counter, looking so deep in thought, so immensely distracted, that it was as if he wasn't present.

Physically? Yes. Mentally? No.

And honestly same. Until he came in.

"One more thing," I added.

God, I'm about to make a fool out of myself.

"Did you hear about the guy who invented the knock knock joke?"

He stared at me very confused, but snapped back into reality.

"He won the no-bell prize."

He bowed his head and started shaking it. I almost couldn't see the hint of a smile that graced his lips.

"Sorry, that joke sucked. I just wanted to make you smile, you looked like you need it."

Something in his stance changed. He looked more relaxed.

"You're total is $2.37," I chirped.

"Here," he didn't break eye contact with me as he held out a ten dollar bill.

"You're change comes out to-"

"Keep it."

"Are you sure?"

"Yes."

"May I ask why?"

The only person that ever tips me is Eleanor.

"You were kind. That means something."

"Thank you. But I don't think that's the real reason. It's just because I tell good jokes."

He just deadpanned at me and walked out the door.

I laughed as he left. I could have sworn I heard him chuckle too.

~~~
~~~

Chapter 2 - Mixed Bat Signals

Chapter Song: Hot N Cold by Katy Perry

EvelynTuesdays are weird.

One gets over the specific type of existential dread that can only occur on Sunday nights before the start of the week.

After Monday is conquered, then it's Tuesday. No one ever says, "Oh thank God it's Tuesday."

No. They say, "it's only Tuesday?"

I absolutely hated Tuesdays with a burning passion when I was in high school. Then again, in high school, every day felt like a Tuesday.

Honestly, the last thing anyone wants to do is wake up at six a.m. to go to first period Spanish and hear their teacher yell "HOLA CLASE!"

Now I stand in front of my mirror before work with a certain kind of peace and gratitude that I'm not in first period Spanish.

~~~
~~~

Clairo's Beachside Cafe was never busy on Tuesdays, especially in summertime, my favorite time of the year. There was no school, just freedom and two and a half months of bliss. And good weather too.

I can't help but stare out of the storefront window at the beach not half a mile from where I stand. Maybe I'd sit on the sand with my toes in the water after work. I'm dressed for it anyway.

Today's warm weather allowed for me to be flexible with my outfit. I put on a white Riley collared tank top and a pair of light blue denim shorts with a light brown belt. I've found that that shirt looks very flattering with my black apron.

Honestly, it's not easy to find an outfit that works for me when I'm five foot two. The proportions are always off. The length of shirts and pants are always...wonky. There's really no way to explain it properly. If you know, you know. If you don't, then lucky you.

I like dressing up a little bit for work. I'm not trying to impress anyone, I just want to feel good. And if color coordinating my outfit helps with that, then I'll happily oblige.

And why not romanticize life?

There's so much to focus on that'll get me down, and I just want to be happy.

For example, I set my alarm to go off to the song Golden by Harry Styles every morning. That's a sure fire guarantee that I wake up to something positive.

Even though Leah makes me want to jump into moving traffic sometimes, I love my job. Yes, I hate hate hate customer service, but

I love meeting nice people. Seeing Eleanor every morning or seeing a couple so happy in love makes me happy.

I do wonder about mystery guy sometimes though.

Until I learn his name, I think I'll call him Batman. His voice was deep like Batman and he looked broody like Batman. It just works out perfectly.

It's been three days since I've seen Batman and I wonder how he's doing. Is he feeling better? Did my bad joke scare him away? No, it couldn't have. It was too good.

Just as I start spiraling into a decent of endless possibilities as to where Batman is, he walks in the door.

And he looks pissed.

"Hi again! How can I help you?" I ask cheerfully.

His eyes are just as pretty as I remember.

"I'll have a chocolate muffin and a black coffee."

Black coffee. That explains a lot.

"Sounds good, can I get a name for the order?"

"No."

No? No?

No one has ever refused to give me a name when I ask for one. It's not like I'm asking for his number or anything, which I would take if he gave it to me but that's besides the point. I'm asking for a name for his coffee.

Maybe this is what everyone means when they say people from California are weird. And as someone from California, I can attest to this.

I ring up his order and he pays. No tip this time. Okie dokie. He was probably just being nice last time. It's my bad for misinterpreting anything. And I guess Batman's angry now. Moody much?

"Would you like a copy of your recei-"

No way. He walked out. He just flat out picked up his muffin and coffee and walked outside to the patio.

For the record, I made that muffin this morning and the way he was manhandling the bag made me want to throw the next muffin he orders at his head.

~~~

Batman has come in every day for the last four days and ordered the exact same thing with a grumpy look on his face. I still try and get him to tell me his name, but he hasn't yet. Weird.

I even try and slide in a joke now and then to see if I can crack him but all I get in response is blatant annoyance and deadpans. My jokes are bad, but they're not bad.

Unlike his mood.

He needs to engage in something that brings him even the slightest bit of joy. Like walking on the beach. Or listening to music. Or walking on the beach while listening to music. That's my happy place, maybe it could be his too if he learned basic manners.

You know what? I've had enough.

I walked right up to his table and just looks up and stares at me annoyed. Per usual.

"Why do you always look like that?" I ask.

"Like what?"
~~~

"Like you hate every person in this room."

"That's because I do."

"Why? What did these people do to you?"

"Nothing. Yet."

"You're a pessimist. Every morning you come in, order black coffee, and glare at every single person in the room."

"I don't glare at you," he paused. "Most of the time."

"We'll that's because I tell good jokes. It'd be criminal to be rude."

I could have sworn that I saw him smile.

"Ha! I saw that! So you do have a heart."

"Everyone has a heart."

"Yes, Mr. Specific, everyone does technically have a heart. But not everyone has a heart. You know?"

"Not even a little bit."

"I think you do and you're just not telling me."

Mischief seems to dance across his features. "And why do you think that?"

"You really want to know?" He nods. "That first day we met you looked sad and then I said something stupid and it made you smile. Well, almost smile, close enough. That's two emotions," I held up two fingers for emphasis. "So I know for a fact that you're capable of showing at least four emotions."

"What are the other two?"

"Anger and irritation."

He chuckled and shook his head. "You're something else."

"If you mean that in a good way, thank you. If you meant that backhandedly, then thank you as well. Now, I'm going to get back to doing my job."

I started to turn around and walk away until I remembered something. "Oh, Batman," he looked around then stared at me confused. "Yes, you. Since you won't tell me your name I came up with my own nickname for you. I think you and Batman share many of the same qualities."

He opened his mouth to say something but I cut him off before he could. "Do stop glaring at the customers. You're going to scare everyone away and I'll lose my job."

He have me a thumbs up before picking up his coffee cup and leaning back in his chair.

Well. That was interesting.

~~~
~~~

Chapter 3 - Gaslighted Hearing

Chapter Song: This Charming Man by The Smiths

EvelynI've come to the conclusion that if my AirPods die, I will die as well.

I don't mean dead as in battery dead, which I'm not worried about that since I always carry an extra charger, I mean dead as in stops working entirely. I think I'd die of cardiac arrest before I made it to the store to get a new pair.

I need music to function. Music makes everything better. Bad day? Put on some music. Good day? Put on some music. Any and every day is a music day to me.

But sometimes music is a little bit dangerous because I get so distracted listening to whatever I'm listening to that I can't hear anything and I don't pay attention to where I'm going and-

Collide with the person standing in front of me and cause both of us to go crashing down onto the concrete.

"Ow," I moan with my eyes squeezed shut. Shit, my head hit the ground hard. I think someone was saying my name, but all I could hear was I'm Still Standing by Elton John playing through my AirPods. Well that's ironic because I am not still standing.

Someone started shaking my shoulders gently. I pull out an AirPod to hear a voice I know so swell yet almost never hear.

"Evelyn," Batman sounds concerned, "are you okay?"

"Yeah," I open my eyes and look at him. Oh God. His nose is practically touching mine. "Batman? Please tell me I'm not hallucinating and it's really you."

He blinks at me. "Yeah, it's me."

I smiled sloppily, still a little bit dazed. "Coolio Batman."

"I really hope you called me Batman because that's my nickname and not because you actually think I'm Batman."

I laughed, "No, mystery man, I know you're not actually Bruce Wayne. Unless your name is Bruce Wayne and you're just not telling me. Then this nickname is more fitting than I thought."

He shook his head and smiled. Oh wow, up this close I can see that he has freckles. He's so cute.

"What?" He asked.

"What?" Did I say that out loud?

"Yes."

Shit.

"You think I'm cute?" And suddenly the space in between us seems even slimmer. Our noses were practically touching.

"I do," I breathed. "Are you sure I said that out loud?"

He chuckled and rolled away from me. He sat up and held out his hand, which I took.

"Are you sure you're okay?" He asked as we started walking down the boardwalk towards the parking lot.

"I'm fine, my head just hurts a little bit. It's nothing a few Tylenol and a nice cup of hot chocolate won't fix."

"Hot chocolate? In the middle of summer?"

"Hey, don't judge. Hot chocolate is a good choice at any time of day. And what are you doing here? I thought you hated all things joyful."

"I do. I live in a bat cave of depression and have emerged to spread my misery to everyone else."

I gasped dramatically, "I should've known. And that's the second time you've embraced the nickname. I think you've finally embraced it."

"No, I think you hit your head too hard and are hearing things."

"Are you gaslighting me, Batman?"

"I don't know what you're talking about." He winked.

"I see what you did there. You're funny, why didn't you tell me that?"

"I thought my charming personality have it away."

I burst out laughing. "Ah yes, a true charmer. You put Han Solo to shame."

"I know."

"You know what I know? This is the most I've ever heard you talk. I guess if it takes me nearly getting concussed for us to have a normal conversation then I'll do this more often."

"Please don't."

"Why? Does Batman have a heart?"

"No."

"Mhm."

We walked in silence for a few more minutes before we made it to the parking lot. I almost didn't want to leave. I think I finally might've cracked the icy shell of his...everything.

"Are you okay to drive?"

"I should be. If not, then you'll know when you don't see me tomorrow.

"Funny," he turned to walk away, then stopped. "Drive safe, Evelyn."

"You too, Batman. Be sure to not spread too much misery today."

~~~

"I'm glad to see that you're still alive," Batman greeted.

"Well that's only because I brew good coffee."

"True."

"Do you want your usual?"

He just stared at me as if I knew the answer. Which I do. Classic Batman.

"I have a proposition for you. You get something, I get something. A quid pro quo of some sorts."

"What is it?"
~~~

"I will give you free muffins for the next three days in exchange for your name."

"Why do you want to know my name so bad?"

"Because you won't tell me."

Batman contemplated my words for a minute before he looked up at me, gorgeous green eyes and all.

"I have a counter offer."

"Fire away."

"I'll tell you my name if you do me the honor of giving me your number."

Oh my God.

Oh my God.

My breath caught in my throat and I'm pretty sure my jaw has dropped into oblivion.

"Okay."

"Really?"

"Yes. Can I get a name for the order?"

"Michael."

"Michael," I repeated. "I like that."

"I like you."

Oh my God. I'm a literally puddle on the floor.

When did he get this smooth? I'm so confused. I feel like I missed a few chapters.

I made his coffee and wrote my number on the cup. Just like in the movies. I handed him his depressing black coffee and he faintly smiled when he saw my number.

"Just like in the movies."

Exactly.

He nodded at me and walked out the door with a final statement: "I told you I'd put Han Solo to shame."

Chapter 4 - Whipped Like Cream

Chapter Song: Falling in Love in a Coffee Shop by Landon Pigg

Michael"Michael," Evelyn repeated slowly. "I like that."

She likes my name. She likes my name.

I hate my name. There's nothing interesting about the name Michael. It's boring and basic. And not to mention the level of hatred I have for the nickname Mike. Mike sounds like a douche. Michael sounds like a slightly less douchey guy.

But I like my name when she says it.

I like her.

And now she's staring at me, completely shocked. Why is she looking at me like that? Did I say something wrong? God, I knew I was too forward.

Wait. Did I say that I liked her out loud?

Shiiiiiiiiiit.

And then she started smiling. Her smile is so pretty. Her eyes light up and I feel...I don't know how to describe it. I just feel.

Evelyn shook her head, still smiling, and turned around to make my coffee.

Her braid was coming undone just like that first time I met her.

I'll always remember that day. Her loose braid and white top made her look like an angel. Not to mention her smile. Her beautiful, beautiful smile.

~~~10 days ago

I was having a shit morning and my shitty coffee machine broke and the even shittier cafe by my apartment was closed, so the next best thing for me was a cafe 3 miles away.

And I'm the idiot who decided to walk there rather than go without coffee.

As I follow the directions on my phone, I can't help but notice how much bird shit there is on the sidewalk.

Not to mention the people walking in front of me who are moving so immensely slow. If my car battery wasn't dead then maybe I'd run over them.

Kidding.

Maybe.

I'm pissed and hungry when I open the door to the cafe. Clairo's Beachside Cafe? Who the fuck names their child Clairo? It's like someone couldn't decide whether to name their child Claire or whatever the hell else they were thinking of.
~~~

"Hi, welcome! How can I-" she stopped talking but I wasn't paying attention. "How can I help you?"

"I'll have a chocolate muffin."

Yes, chocolate. Maybe it'll bring me some semblance of joy. I didn't want to get a call from my brother this morning. He only calls when he's drunk or wants money. And his words always hurt. I know I shouldn't listen, but I can't help but replay every word he says over and over until I wish that I wasn't what he said I am.

Because he's right. He's right that I'm a disappointment and that I'm a heartless piece of shit.

"One more thing."

I looked up at the barista and there was something about her that just made me stop. She noticed that she had my attention and humor danced in her dark eyes.

"Did you hear about the guy who invented the knock knock joke?"

What the hell? No, I didn't fucking hear about the guy who invented the knock knock joke. Who even knows anything about that?

I'm not in the mood for this right-

"He won the "no bell" prize."

Why would he win the nobel-

Oh.

That was a joke.

I deadpan at her and I see her smile. Then I smile.

Why am I smiling?

I mean that was a good joke but it wasn't that good.

"Sorry," she said into the silence. Probably because I wasn't saying anything. "That joke sucked. I just wanted to make you smile, you looked like you needed it."

Oh. Why? Was it that obvious? Knowing my RBF, it probably was, but why try and help? She doesn't even know me. I just stare at her, unable to speak.

"You're total is $2.37," she chirped.

"Here," I didn't, I couldn't, break eye contact with her as I held out a ten dollar bill.

"You're change comes out to-"

"Keep it."

Shock flashed in her eyes. "Are you sure?"

"Yes."

"May I ask why?"

"You were kind. That means something."

"Thank you. But I don't think that's the real reason. It's just because I tell good jokes."

I heard her laugh as I left. Why was her laugh so pretty? It was just so contagious and unburdened that I laughed too.

I walked out with a kind of liveliness that coffee could never give me.

~~~

She gives me my coffee and it's burning hot, but I don't care. I've been waiting for this moment. I've been trying to build up the courage to ask her for her number for ten days now and I haven't been able to. Until today.
~~~

And now her number is on the top of my cup.

I chuckle, "just like in the movies."

And. She. Smiles. Again.

Why does she keep doing that?

She needs to stop or else she'll have me smiling like an idiot too.

I feel like I'm talking about her smile a lot.

It's just so pretty and her eyes get all sparkly and-

Shit.

I'm so whipped.

~~~

HEYYYYYYYMichael's POV was so much fun to write. He's all grumpy and sweet, it's so cute. I just found out that Starbucks has white hot chocolate and my life has forever been changed.
~~~

Chapter 5 - Diners, Drive-Ins and Dies

Chapter Song: Summer on You by PRETTYMUCH

EvelynThe beauty of living alone in a one bedroom apartment is that I can do whatever I want and decorate it however I so choose to.

That's probably the only two upsides to this apartment.

I say this with all of the love in my heart, my apartment is trash. Again, with all of the love in my heart. I mean, the power goes out sometimes and so does the heating and now that I think about it the AC too, but at least I have somewhere to live. I'd rather live here than somewhere else. It may be a piece of trash, but it's my piece of trash.

If anything, I relate the my apartment. Running on fumes sometimes but still going with all of its effort. If anything, it's courageous. And I feel like I could use some courage.

Before my father died, he would tell me that I'll get nowhere in life with my personality. He said I was too annoying and too much of a failure to amount to anything.

He told me that it was my fault my mom died. I told myself he wrong about a lot of things, but he was right about that. It's my fault. He made sure that I'd never forget that, but in all honestly, I'd never let myself forget.

I was snapped out of my thoughts by the sound of my phone buzzing. I checked it and it was an unknown number.

Unknown: Hey EvUnknown: It's Michael

Oh shit.

Michael texted me. Michael's texting me. What do I do?

Okay, play it cool.

Me: Hi!!!!

Four exclamation marks? Really?

Michael : I have a questionMichael : Where did Batman come from

Me: Gotham

Michael : I meant the nickname you gave me

Me: OhMe: HahaMe: It's because you remind me of him

Michael : Why?

Me: Because you brood

Michael : I don't

Me: Are you scowling at your phone right now?

Michael : ...

Me: My point exactlyMe: You know, I've been writing Batman as the call name on your coffee cup every morning, I can't decide whether I want to change it to Michael or not

Michael : You can change it

Me: I have an good idea

Michael : No

Me: Don't shut it down so fast!

Michael : I already did

Me: RudeMe: But I won't back downMe: You'll see tomorrow. Okay?

Michael : Fine

He's going to love it.

~~~

"Coffee for Michael," I called.

It was unnaturally busy for a Thursday (which is strange because our coffee isn't even that good) and I didn't have time to talk to Michael this morning. The most I talked to him was getting his order and calling his name for the coffee. I was kind of sad that wouldn't get to see his reaction to the present I left on his cup.

Since it was so busy, all of the customers were bumping into each other. It was kind of funny.

Although, what really brightened my mood was seeing Michael react to his surrounding. It was almost like watching Ron from Parks and Recreation when he was annoyed. Or at any time of the day.
~~~

Some random guy bumped into Michael as he was walking out the door and Michael slowly turned around and glared at him like he just committed the worst crime known to mankind.

It was hilarious.

~~~

By the end of my shift I considered quitting. Only one thing stopped me from doing so: I need the money. I like working there, don't get me wrong, but it's just not where I want to be. I want to be in a bookstore and read all day. But that doesn't pay the bills. So I'm here.

Ooo Michael texted me.

10:20Michael : I know it's busy right now at your work, but do you want to get lunch after your shift?

Wait, what time is it now? 1:30. Already? I feel like I've been in that caffeine serving coffin for years.

Lunch sounds amazing, actually. I'm starving.

Me: That sounds great! What time?

"How about now?" I hear someone ask once I stepped out of the cafe. I spin around to see Michael. Sitting on a bench.

"Michael? How'd you know when I got off my shift?"

"I didn't."

"How long have you been sitting here for?"

He checked his watch, "three hours."

"Three hours? Why?"

"I wanted to have lunch with you."

"I understand that, but why?"
~~~

He chuckled, "Is there anything specific you want to eat?"

"Tacos."

"Tacos?"

"Yes, tacos. Spicy tacos, to be specific."

"Really?"

Is that a hint of fear I detect in his voice?

"Yes, really. Why, is that a problem for you?"

"No," he replied abruptly.

Oh, he's so scared.

~~~

"Are you sure this is even safe to eat?" Michael asked as he eyes the sample tray I got us to try. I took him to this cute food truck that had the best tacos. And the spiciest.

Our tray consisted of tacos with chicken or beef and several toppings like cilantro, onions, tomato, etc. All of the meats were seasoned, but not spicy. The spice lied in the sauces. There were seven different levels of spice labeled from "whimp" to "Satan himself."

"Yeah! I eat this all the time. You should be fine."

"I seriously doubt it," I hear him mutter.

"What was that?"

"Nothing."

"If you don't want to eat the spiciest level, you don't have to. I don't even do it. My max is six. But that's when I'm feeling brave. I feel like I'm eating fire with that one, I don't know how people eat level 8."

Michael just started at me dumbfounded before clearing his throat, "I'll start with two. Work my way up."
~~~

"That seems reasonable."

Michael tentatively took a bite. It was so funny, he was processing the flavor with such a deep level of concentration that could only be equivalent to defusing a bomb.

"Are you okay?" I asked slowly.

"Yeah," he replied, somehow talking slower than I had. "That wasn't bad."

"I would hope not, that's only level two. People start to feel the burn around level 4."

"I'll try level 5."

"Are you sure?" I ask bewildered. "That's pretty hot."

"I'm sure. What's the name for that one."

"Dancing in Hellfire."

"That's not frightening at all. What's yours called?"

"Since it's the next step up, Drowning in Hellfire."

"Who comes up with this stuff?"

"I don't know, but I want to be their friend. Now, stop stalling. Go for it."

Michael was about to take a bite, then he paused. "On one condition."

"Alright."

"If I eat this, can I plan what we do next?"

"Like a date?"

"No, not yet. But, if you'll let me, soon."

I smiled, "Yes. To both."

Michael's lips quirked up into a surprises smile.

"Now that the stakes have been set, eat."

Michael suspiciously eyes his taco one last time before he took a much bigger bite then I expected. He winced as if bracing himself for pain. After a moment he peeled one of his eyes open and started, "That wasn't too-"

And then he started coughing. His face turned as red as the Satan Himself sauce and he reached for his water. Michael chugged the whole bottle and didn't look like he was doing any better.

"That didn't help," he wheezed, tears in his eyes.

I couldn't take it any longer. I started laughing. No, not laughing, cackling.

"Why," I asked in between breaths, "Did you use so much sauce?"

I pushed a medium sized carton of milk across the table to Michael, who looked like he was about to light on fire. He eagerly drank it before sighing in relief.

"I didn't think it'd be that bad."

"You didn't," I wheezed, "Think it'd be that bad? It's called Dancing in Hellfire, Michael. It's going to be bad."

"Well," Michael stated defensively, "at least now I get to choose what we do next."

"I look forward to it."

"Me too," Michael said softly.

~~~

HEYYYYYYYI believe that the people who can eat spicy food are going to live longest until the zombie apocalypse. I can't pinpoint why, exactly, but I just get that feeling.And RIP Michael. He really
~~~

went through all six stages of grief eating that taco. Thank you for the support on the story!

Chapter 6 - Indicision and an Irrational Desire to Throw Out Half of my Clothes

Chapter Song: Primadonna by MARINA

(I chose this song because I picture Evelyn dramatically singing and dancing to this while getting ready for her date.)

EvelynI don't know what to wear.

Michael texted me and told me to meet him at the local flower shop. He said that he'd "meet me in the front but we'd only be able to hang out for about five minutes."

I'm a little bit confused, but intrigued.

So, essentially, I have to choose an outfit that is simple, but not too simple where it looks like I didn't try. But it can't be too dressy or over the top because this isn't a date and I'm only meeting with him for a few minutes.

Screw it, I'll just wear sweats.

~~~

I am currently wearing jean shorts and ruffled black t-shirt with daisies on it. So, not exactly sweats.

Michael told me to meet at 2 o'clock, but it's 2:05 and he's not here. Maybe he's late. That's okay, it happens to the best of us. Or maybe he's inside? I make the decision to look through the storefront window and it's the best decision I've ever made.

Michael, wearing a green apron and disheveled hair, is standing next to a man who is admiring a bouquet of roses.

No way.

Michael works here? That's awesome. I am pleasantly surprised, I wouldn't have pegged him for the working in a flower shop kind of guy.

I think it's adorable.

The customer pays for his flowers and walks out the door. Michael tilts his head back and sighs, a small smile on his face. I decide to look away before he catches me and text him saying I'm outside.

Me: Hey BatmanMe: I'm outside the shopBatman :...Batman : I'm so sorry I'm late. I'll be right there

Sure enough, less than twenty seconds later I hear the bell ring and Michael walks out. Somehow, he looks even more disheveled than he was a few minutes ago.

He looks at me surprised and says, "You showed up."

"Of course! Why wouldn't I?"
~~~

"Never mind. I wanted to take a little bit more time to do this properly, but I only have," he checked his watch. "Two minutes.

"I like you. I think you're really kind and," he stopped, shaking his head. "Honestly, I have no idea why you talk to me. It doesn't make sense. But I, uh, I like it when you talk to me. And I would like to take you out on a date. If that's okay with you."

I smiled at him, "I'd love to go on a date with you."

"Really?"

"Yes," I laughed. "Really."

He sighed, running his left hand through his hair and relaxing a little bit. I hadn't realized how tense he was until now.

"Here." He moved his right hand from behind his back and held out a cluster of beautiful, vibrant flowers for me to take. It was purplish blue and had a little bit of yellow on it. There was a little yellow ribbon tied around the stem in the shape of a cute bow.

"They're irises. They represent wisdom, cherished friendship, and hope. They're nicknamed 'the dancing spirit.' And they," he looked down. "They remind me of you."

I'm speechless. I've never been speechless, but I'm speechless.

"I-" I can't even come up with the words to describe how I feel, what I want to say.

"Do you like them? If not then that that's okay this is stupid, really-"

"Michael," I interrupt. "I love them. I love them so much I don't know what I want to say. No one's ever done something so kind for me. Thank you."

"It's no problem, really. I wanted to." His watch beeped and he checked it. "Shit, I have to get back. Does Friday at 8 work for you?"

"Yes, that sounds great."

"Perfect. I'll see you tomorrow. Uh, bye." He went inside with an awkward nod of his head and I smiled the rest of the day.

~~~

I stared at the irises that have a new home on my desk. I don't know how he knew, but irises are my favorite flower.

He put so much thought into picking the flowers, and all of that thought...was of me. He was thinking about me.

Why? Because he cares? No, he doesn't. People don't care. They leave and they make you feel worthless.

But maybe not everyone is like that.

Maybe Michael's different.

So far, he's off to a great start. I can only hope that sometime I'll be able to make him as happy as he did when he gave me the irises.

~~~

Lavender is my favorite color. I love shades of purple, but there's something just so pretty about lavender. It's calm and comforting yet playful at the same time.

In my humble and bias opinion, it's the best color.

That's why I chose a lavender sun dress for my date tonight.

Michael is supposed to pick me up anytime now and I look in the mirror one last time. My hair is done half up with a waterfall braid and loose waves fall over my shoulders. I accented the outfit with a gold necklace and a gold ring that looks like vines.

The doorbell rang.

Michael.

I opened the door and there he was. He stood wearing a light blue button up shirt and black jeans.

He looked so pretty.

~~~

HEYYYYYYYYOkay, this is shorter than I planned. I wanted to make it long and combine Chapters 6 and 7, but I'm switching the POV next chapter and I don't like switching POVS mid chapter. And now you guys have more content haha. Sorry for the filler chapter. I've already started the next one and I'm so excited. It's going to be soooooo cute. I'm looking forward to you guys reading it!And I'd like to give a special shout-out toThank you for your support since the very beginning, I appreciate it!
~~~

Chapter 7 - Not Even Shakespear Could Write Anyone as Perfect as You

Chapter Song: Yellow by Coldplay

MichaelEvelyn is the most beautiful girl I've ever seen.

I can't describe it. She's just...radiant.

Why? Why does she all always make me feel...things. I don't like it. I actually fucking hate it. But here I am.

And here she is.

Evelyn looks beautiful in everything she wears, but lavender is her color. Her dress fit her perfectly, it was almost as if it was made for her.

I meet her gaze and she looks away, a slight blush settling on her cheeks.

Is she shy? She has no reason to be.

"You look beautiful, Ev."

"Thank you. You look pretty too."

Fuck.

"Are you ready to go?" I asked, clearing my throat.

"Yeah, let's do it."

~~~

"Close your eyes."

"Why?" Evelyn asked, puzzled. We were walking up a hill and I didn't want her to see what I had planned at the top yet.

"Just trust me."

"Trust you, Batman? Always."

I smiled and she closed her eyes.

"May, I?" I asked, my arm outstretched towards her.

"May you what, Michael? I can't see what you're doing."

Oh. Right.

"I don't want you to fall, so may I take your arm and guide you to where we're going?"

"Such a gentleman."

Evelyn outstretched her arm and I looped it in mine, walking us up to the top of the hill.

Then she continued talking. "You asked if I trusted you, I said yes. But I'm just now realizing that was naive of me. I mean, you could be an axe murder and you're just leading me to my death."

I lifted an eyebrow, "Do you really think that I'm an axe murder?"

"I don't know, that's the whole point. If you are, then you have some very good and elaborate planning to get me out here. You can easily murder me since it's dark, I'm uncoordinated, and I'm wearing sandals so God knows I won't be able to run away."
~~~

Even though she thinks I might be an axe murderer, which I take mild offense to, I don't mind. Listening to her, I don't want her to stop.

I never want her to stop talking, smiling, and being the sun, the moon, and stars.

"All I ask," she confused. "Is that you feed my fish when I'm gone. Don't eat him, though. He's just a beta fish, so he wouldn't make a good lunch, or even a snack, at that."

"I didn't know you have a fish."

"His name is Wasabi."

I blink, "I'm sorry, did you say Wasabi?"

"I did."

That's fucking precious.

"I don't eat sushi in front him though. So if you kill me, don't do that either."

"I won't."

"So you do plan to take me into the woods and murder me. I should've known. I'm hurt, really, but I can accept it."

"Shut up," I say playfully. "I need to concentrate, we're just about there."

I carefully navigate the two of us to the picnic. Before I picked her up, I set up a small picnic. I didn't know what she liked, so I got everything. Everyone likes bread, so I brought bread, butter, cheese, grapes, and apple cider, since I didn't know exactly how old she was. She looked twenty or twenty one maybe? I just didn't want to be insensitive.

I placed a few irises in a little plastic cup in the middle of the blanket.

I hope she likes it.

I let go of her arm and step behind her, "You can open your eyes now."

I hear her breath catch in her throat. Evelyn looks down at the picnic and I wish I knew what she was thinking.

Does she not like it? Does she like it? Why is this so fucking nerve racking?

Then we see it at the same time. A shooting star flies across the sky.

Still behind her, I see her head shoot up. Then the next star passes. And then the next. And the next. There's so many because they're not stars, they're meteors.

"How," she whispers, still looking up. "How did you do this? How did you know?"

"You like to wear earrings with little stars on them. I thought this might be nice."

And once I saw that I checked to see when the next meteor shower was because I knew that's where I wanted to take you.

I wanted to see you under the moonlight with a million stars dancing around us but I can't see you because you haven't turned around yet which is making me lose my mind because I want to know what you think-

And then she turned around.

I lost my breath and found it in the same moment.

Evelyn looked breathtaking. The moonlight made her skin glow and the very stars above us danced in her wondering eyes.

Secretly, I envy the stars for being the thing that's receiving her stare.

But that envy doesn't last long because now she's staring at me.

All of the awe and joy in her eyes was now directed at me and I think I'm dying. I don't think it's possible to feel how I feel right now and still be alive.

Her smile grew brighter and she stared at me like I was one in the same with the very stars she adored.

Catching me completely off gaurd, she ran into my arm holding me right.

"Thank you," she whispered. "Thank you so much."

I wrapped my arms around her, and leaned my head into the top of her hair. She smelled like oranges. "Of course."

Anything for you.

She pulled away slightly to look up at me.

Wow, her eyes are so pretty. They're so dark that before I know it I'll find myself lost in them for hours.

"This is perfect. I don't know how to thank you for this."

"You already have."

"How?" Evelyn asked.

"Just you being here. Taking a chance on me."

"Yeah, you're grumpiness didn't scare me away." She patted my shoulder once and sat down on the blanket.

"So," she started, popping a grape in her mouth. "What's your favorite animal?"

"An octopus."

"An octopus?"

"Yeah. What about you?"

"Capybaras."

"They're cute and kinda funky. I like them."

I chuckled and pulled out the bottle of apple cider, "Here, I got cider."

We sat and talked about so much. I learned a few things about her too.

1.) Her birthday is July 24th and she is almost 21. 2.) She scrolls on TikTok or reads until really early in the morning most nights.3.) Her biggest pet peeve is people talking during a movie. 4.) Her favorite color is lavender.

After we ate and talked some more, we sat in a comfortable silence, staring at the meteor shower and enjoying each other's company.

And then I heard a clicking sound.

"What's that?" Evelyn asked.

After maybe three more clicks, the sprinklers turned on.

Evelyn screamed and started laughing, jumping off the ground in a futile attempt to try and get less wet.

"Why the fuck are there sprinklers in a park?" I yelled over her laughter and the sprinklers.

"How else will the grass stay green?" She yelled back.

"Oh yeah."

We grabbed the now completely soaked blanket and ran, no, slipped, down the hill towards my car before the sprinklers at the bottom of the hill turned on too.

By the time we got into my car, I was soaking wet and happy beyond comprehension.

~~~

HEYYYYYYYYYY!I'm back! Sorry for the delay, it was another brutal school week. You get it. I am so happy to put this out to you guys. The alternate picture was going to be a picture of Wasabi, who I adore already. After writing this I came to the conclusion that I'm going to die alone.Okay, enjoy!!!!!!
~~~

Chapter 8 - Melatonin Munchies

Chapter Song: Vulnerable by Selena Gomez

EvelynThat was the best date of my life. I don't think any date will ever top that; It was perfect.

While we were running from the sprinklers, which honestly was insanely comical, I took one of the irises from the cup.

Now I've set it on my desk and I can't help but feel like it might be my new favorite flower. And maybe, just beyond that, maybe I have a new favorite person. I know it's early, but we've known each other for two months and when I'm with him I just...feel.

I feel joy, comfort, and safety. It's refreshing and, if I'm being completely honest, it's new.

If Wasabi possessed the ability to speak, I'm sure we'd have a long conversation about this.

But he doesn't, so I guess my only consultation will be myself.

Shit, it's cold in my apartment.

I have such a bad immune system, I wouldn't doubt it if I catch a cold or something. Knowing my luck, I probably will.

I think I'll just pop a few melatonin gummies for some good sleep and eat an orange for the vitamin C.

That should work.

In theory.

If not, at least I'll die happy.

~~~

"Are you okay?" Michael asked. "You said you needed to vent."

"You'll never guess what happened."

"What happened?"

I told Michael I wanted to meet him for lunch. It's been three days since our date and I've never been happier. Except for an hour ago.

"So," I started. "This guy came in to order a coffee, his name is Brad."

"Sounds like a douche."

"For sure. I gave him his order and he said I made his coffee wrong. Which, for the record, was just black coffee, so there is no way I made it wrong. I've been a barista for two years, I think I know how to brew a pot of coffee. But that's beside the point.

"I asked him if he wanted me to remake the drink completely free of charge and he said 'no, but now you have to live with the fact that you messed up my coffee. I hope you sleep restlessly."

"The fuck?"

"I know! And he just walked out after that. Like, what even?"

"I don't have words."
~~~

"I have a quite a few actually, but I'm my effort to be a good person I won't share them."

Michael chuckled. I love his chuckle. It's not a full laugh, but it's enough. And the way his lips quirk up into the smallest of smiles is so adorable. He's so-

I sneezed.

I just sneezed the world's most horrific sneeze and I think I'm going to die of embarrassment.

Ugh, I felt that in my soul.

"Bless you?"

"Oh," I laughed nervously, "thanks."

Michael looked at me part concerned and part perplexed when he asked, "Are you okay?"

"Me? Oh yeah, I'm fine. It's probably just allergies."

Or my immune system sucks.

Or I've been up really late scrolling on TikTok every night for the past week and haven't gotten much sleep.

Or maybe I should've had two oranges instead of one with my melatonins two night ago.

I think I'll try that tonight, see what happens.

"Ev?"

"Yeah," I snapped my head up to look at him.

"I lost you for a second. You good?"

"Oh yeah, I was just thinking that I need to get some food for Wasabi. I used the last of it this morning."

"Do you want to go now?"

"I've got nothing better to do."

~~~

"Why are there so many different types of fish food?" Michael asked, staring at the wall of betta fish food.

"Don't be fooled, Batman. They're all the exact same just in different colors. I buy the rainbow one to spice up Wasabi's boring life."

Michael raised an eyebrow.

"I mean, when it comes down to it, fish are doomed to live in an endless cycle of swimming in the exact same tank for the entirety of their lives. It's the same concept as corporate mediocrity except the fish can't escape."

Michael stared at me absolutely bewildered.

"What?"

"I don't know exactly."

I playfully punched his arm, "Come on, I know you know what you want to say."

"Yeah, I think I do: Not to sound like a broken record, but are you okay?"

"Always and never," I winked. "But I am always okay when I'm with you, so I'll take that as a win. Now come on, let's pay for this and then we can go to my apartment and feed Wasabi."

~~~

"My apartment is kind of a mess," I started as I wiggled my key inside the lock. "So please don't judge."

"I won't. Do you-uh-need help with that?"

"This?" I motioned to the lock which still wouldn't unlock. "I'm okay, thanks. This happens sometimes. You kind of just have to jiggle it a bit for it to open."

"Is that safe?"

"Absolutely not."

After their more seconds of trying, the door clicked open. "Yes! Suck it, shitty door."

I turned the lights on and all of a sudden I was self conscious. I didn't think about it before, but what would Michael think?

My apartment is my home and sharing it is a certain type of vulnerability I didn't even consider when I invited him over.

My interest, my personality, my biggest insecurities are written all over the walls.

He can see my Harry Styles posters, all of my books, the little glass animals I keep on my windowsill, the absolute lack of food in my pantry. Everything, every bit of my personality is laid exposed for him tear apart if he chooses to.

I've found that now, watching him take in the room, I can't breath. He's going to hate it. It's too much. Just like me. I should've known this would be it for him, I'm too much it's all-

"It reminds me of you."

I snap my head up to look at him. "What does?"

"Everything," he said, completely awestruck. "It all reminds me of you."

"In a bad way?"

"What?" He turned and took my hands in his. "No, why would you think that?"

I bowed my head and shrugged, "I guess I'm just used to it."

"Ev, it reminds me of you in the best way. Your energy and joy and passion. It's all here and it's all you. Every fun, beautiful part."

I couldn't help my smile for the rest of the evening.

~~~

HEYYYYYYYYYI promise that now I'll be posting more than I was beforeI didn't spell check this because I'm about to start the next chapter and I'm excited. So sorry for any mistakes hahaI have so much planned for the next few chapters. It's about to get gooooooooood-Enjoy everyone!
~~~

Chapter 9 - Off to the Asylum I Go

Chapter Song: It May Sound Strange by Spencer Sutherland

MichaelI need coffee.

I simply just can't function without coffee. And it's already been a shitty morning, so that's great.

My fucking brother tried calling me again and I'm ten seconds away from blocking his number.

I just want to have a quiet day, is that really too much to ask for?

Well, there might be something that'll help me.

Evelyn.

I start my car and stare at the passenger seat for solid minute. I can still see her there, from that night. Smiling and laughing while she slammed the door shut so the sprinklers wouldn't get the inside of the car wet too.

Even as I'm driving, I can hear her singing along to whatever song came on the radio. Somehow she knew all of them.

I think I'll ask her out again today. See if she wants to go to the movies or something.

Maybe we could see Batman.

But I won't be able to see her if this asshole in front of me won't move at the green light.

I honked and stuck my head out the car window, "Hey asshole!"

The guy in the car turned around, confused.

"Yeah, you," I continued. "It's a green light."

He waved and drove away.

I hate people.

Just like this. It's a green light, that means go, as everyone knows. And what was he doing? Not going.

It's the same thing as a group of people who walk slow and in a horizontal line in the middle of a crowded hallway. It's just so annoying.

~~~

I walk in and am greeted by the familiar smell of freshly brewed coffee.

I look at the counter and Evelyn isn't here.

I pull out my phone, it's 10:34. should be here by now, her shift started at 9 o'clock.

I have a bad feeling. Maybe it's my absence of coffee or my shitty morning, but I just have a bad feeling.

Okay, think rationally. Maybe she's just getting something from the back storage or something.
~~~

I walk up to the counter and one of the baristas practically runs up to greet me. She staring me weird. I don't like it. "Hi, how can I help you?"

"I was wondering if Evelyn is here today?"

"Oh," the barista said, moderately annoyed. "Evelyn. Yeah, she never showed up for her shift this morning."

"Did she call out or tell anyone why she didn't come in?"

"Nope." Then she eyed me suspiciously,as if now she was relaxing I was grilling her for information. "Why do you want to know?"

I don't know why but my heart starts racing, is she okay? Is something wrong?

"She's my...friend. And I just got worried when I didn't see her. Thanks for the help."

I walked out and sat in my car. I sent her a text.

Me: Hey Ev, are you okay? I saw you weren't at work

Nothing. Not a single thing. I wait for five minutes.

Me: Ev?

Five more minutes. Still nothing.

I try calling her.

Calling Ev ...

...

...

...

Ev: Hi! This is Evelyn!Me: Ev! I'm so happy you're-Ev: I can't come to the phone right now, so please leave a message after the beep and I'll get back to you as soon as I can!

Shit.

It's just a voicemail.

She never misses work, she hates being late, and she always responds to a text or call, even if it's just to say that she can't talk at the moment.

I don't know, I just have a bad feeling.

~~~

"Ev?" I lightly knocked on her door. "Are you there?"

Nothing. I'll text her again. Maybe she can't hear me.

Me: Ev?

Then I hear it. Her phone pings from somewhere on the other side of the door.

I try calling her.

I hear her groan and some rustling on the end of the door.

She picks up

"Hello?"

I sigh, letting out a deep breath.

"Hey Ev, it's me."

"Michael?"

Wow, she sounds exhausted.

"Yeah, Ev, it's me. Are you okay?"

...

"Ev?"

"Yeah, sorry. I think my allergies are all out of wack. I'm kind of tired."

"That's okay. Can I come in?"
~~~

"Yeah, let me just-" she started coughing. "Let me just unlock the door."

She hung up and I heard the door click unlocked before she opened it.

Oh my God. She looks like shit.

She looks beautiful, as always, but also like shit.

Her hair is kind of all over the place and her usual glowing skin is pale and blotchy. She looks so tired too, the evidence of a bad nights sleep is written all over her face.

"Ev, I say this with all of the kindness in my heart, but you look like shit."

She laughed and turned around gesturing for me to follow her inside.

"Shit, Ev," I said, closing the door. "It's freezing in here."

"Yeah, the AC or heating unit or whatever controls this apartment sucks. It's either always way too hot or way to cold. I get lucky if it's somewhere in the middle."

She plopped down on her bed, gesturing for me to sit next to her. She has a little blanket fort set up and she started to swaddle herself in blankets.

"Do you want to watch anything? I was just watching The Great British Baking Show but I can change it if you want."

I just started at her, completely speechless. A little bit confused too. With the way she looks right now, I don't even know how she's conscious.

"Why are you looking at me like that?"

"Like what?"

"Like you're worried."

"Do you normally feel like this when your allergies are bad?"

"No," she said with her eyes closed.

I lifted my hand up to feel her forehead. "Shit, sweetheart, your burning up."

"Am I?"

"Yeah."

Wait.

Did I just?

No, I'm hallucinating. I have to be. There's no way I just-

I wasn't trying to say that it just...came out.

I liked how it sounded though.

I cleared my throat, "Evelyn, I think you have a fever."

She groaned, rolling to her side and bundling up even more in the blankets. "You have a fever," she mumbled.

I smiled, "What?"

"You heard me."

Out of nowhere there was a loud sputtering sound from beneath Evelyn's window. Her AC box turned on? How? It was already so cold in here, I can't imagine it getting colder.

And now a dog is barking downstairs.

Almost as if in response, Evelyn pulled the blankets over her head.

"Is it always this loud in here?"

I saw her head nod from under the covers. "I usually put in my AirPods to drown out the sound, but they're dead."

"Ev?" I said softly. "You're apartment is really nice, but it being so cold and loud in here is definitely not helping your fever. You need to rest."

"I'll be fine," she mumbled. "I actually have to go to the market so I can make food. So I'll get a break from the noise."

I sighed, what is she thinking? I guess fever delirium is real.

"I would highly advise that you don't do that. I think you'll pass out."

"I don't want to be in my apartment anymore though. And I need food," she whined.

"How about this: If you want a change in scenery, we can go to my apartment. It's quiet there and I can make you some soup."

"How sweet of you. Let's do it."

~~~

I tried to get Evelyn to walk over to the bed but she pretty much passed out one the couch.

"Ev," I nudged her slightly. "Do you want tea?"

"Yes, please."

I walked over to the coffee pot, which I haven't used since I met her, and started brewing the coffee. I walked to the couch and sat down next to her. She repositioned so that her head was resting on my thigh.

Looking up at me, she said, "I think I know why I'm sick."

My eyebrows furrowed together, "Why?"

"The customer yesterday, he told me that he hoped I would sleep restlessly. Now I wake up with a fever. It's all Brad's fault."
~~~

"Fucking Brad."

She smiled and hummed before closing her eyes again. She was sound asleep in less than a minute.

I brushed a loose strand of hair out of her face and I couldn't help but stare at her.

Her hair was so soft and, even totally passed out and sick, she still smelled like oranges. I wish I could just hold her like this forever.

It's so stupid.

It is so stupid that someone can just push their way into someone's every thought and make them crazy.

I think a little craziness can't hurt.

And if feeling whatever it is that I feel when I'm with her makes me crazy, then lock me up in an asylum because I'm not going to stop.

Knock knock knock.

Who the fuck is knocking on my door?

I leave look down at Evelyn and she stirs slightly, but doesn't wake up.

Knock knock knock.

Evelyn moves a little bit more, burying herself further under the blankets.

Shit, that's not going to stop.

Slowly, I got up, making sure I was careful not to wake her up.

I tiptoed to the door and opened it.

No.

No.

How the fuck did he find my apartment?

"Hey Michael," my brother teased, coyly. "How are things?"

~~~

HEYYYYYYYYYYYTHANK YOU SO MUCH FOR 1,000 VIEWS! It's a surreal feeling to be honest

Poor Evelyn, I do firmly believe that her fever is all Brad's fault-Michael is just a ready bear and a sweetie for taking care of Evelyn. After yet another chapter in his POV, I stand by my statement that I'm going to die aloneAnd so we meet the brother *insert maniacal laughter*Things are heating up!

And an informal shoutout to everyone who's commented their support for the book so far! Even if you haven't commented and just read, I appreciate a lot! You all rock!
~~~

Chapter 10 - Forgotten Tea

Chapter Song: Little Things by One Direction

Michael"What the fuck are you doing here?"

"What?" Derek smiled. "I can't stop by to say hello to my favorite brother?"

"No. Get out."

"I see you haven't lost your charm."

I think I'm going to punch him.

"How did you find my apartment?" I asked.

I haven't seen my brother in 3 years and I never told him where I moved. I wanted, want, him completely out of my life.

"Do you really want to know?" Derek teased.

"Actually, no. Just get the fuck out."

"If you bothered to answer my calls, then you'd know why I'm here." He pulled out an envelope and handed it to me. Wearily, I took it.

It was filled with so much cash that I didn't have to count it to know that it was well over a thousand dollars.

"Where did you get this?"

"Business."

"Doing what?"

"Nothing you need to worry about."

I shoved the money into his chest, forcing him to grab it.

"Listen, I don't want to take your dirty money or ve an accessory to-"

Beep beep beep.

The coffee machine.

Shit. That's going to wake her up.

"Don't move, I'll be back."

I closed the door and tiptoed my way past Evelyn and over to the coffee machine. I turned it off and sighed.

Why is he here?

The last time I saw Derek was 5 years ago and he was behind bars after being charged with armed robbery.

He can't be here. I have a life, a home, Evelyn. I can't have him here to make me lose everything again. I can't do it. Not again.

"Who's this?"

I whipped around to see Derek standing over a sleeping Evelyn, his hand moving towards her face.

"Get the fuck away from her."

Derek retracted his hand, looking up at me and smiling, "She's a pretty thing, isn't she?"

"I said," I spoke cold and low, aggression seeping from my tone. "Get the fuck away from her."

"Alright," he walked towards me and into the kitchen.

"I don't want your money," I hissed. "And I sure as hell don't want you anywhere near myself or Evelyn. So get the fuck out of my apartment and don't show your face around here again."

"Alright."

He always says that. I hate it.

I watched as Derek walked towards the front door. He paused with his hand on the door handle.

"One more thing," he turned around slowly, a coy smile pulling at his lips. "Does she always look that intoxicating while she sleeps?"

My hands curled into fists.

The fuck did he just say about her?

"See you soon, Michael."

He slammed the door shut, leaving me fuming.

I'm going to kill him. If I ever see him again, I'm going to kill him.

"Michael?" Evelyn groaned sleepily, sitting up from her position on the couch.

Shit. That asshole woke her up.

"Shhh, I'm here," I walked to the couch, touching my hand to her forehead. She's still burning up.

"Hold on a second, okay?" After getting a nod from Evelyn, I walked over to the kitchen and pulled out a thermometer to take her temperature.

Oh my God, it's 102 degrees.

Should she go to the hospital for that?

"Ev, how are you feeling?"

"I-" Evelyn started coughing again, "I feel awful."

"I'm sorry, sweetheart. Can I get you anything?"

She smiled sloppily, staring up at me.

"What?" I asked.

"I like it when you call me sweetheart."

My heart skipped a beat. She does?

Wait, no, she can't. She's delirious with a 102 degree fever. She can't mean it.

But if she does...

"What if I called you something too? Like darling or sweetheart?" Evelyn asked.

Then I think my heart would melt.

"You already call me sweetheart though," she continued. "So I think darling works."

"Call me darling when you feel better, okay?"

"I can do that."

We sat in silence, staring at the tv yet not really watching. She looked distracted, I don't know what it was, but something was on her mind.

"Michael?" She slurred.

"Yeah?"

"Do you think I'm a burden?"

"What?" I say, breathlessly. "No, of course not. Why would you think that?"

"Because I'm annoying and a waste of space. It'd make sense that you'd think the same as they did."

"Ev, please don't ever talk about yourself like that again. You are kind and fun and best person I've ever met on this fucking planet. So, please, don't think of yourself as anything less."

"I think I'm going to nap again," Evelyn blurted out, changing the subject. "Can you lay with me?"

"Of course," I sighed. We'd definitely need to revisit this conversation when she feels better. "But you really would be more comfortable on the bed."

"I don't want to impose."

"Ev, I insist. You'd probably sleep better too. You'll get better quicker with a good nights sleep."

She nodded her head and started sitting up again. Slowly, we made our way over to my room. My bed wasn't big, but it was large enough to fit us both.

She climbed, or, more accurately, fell, on the bed and pushed the blankets over herself. I got in on the other side and she pushes herself closer to me, resting her head on my arm.

"Sleep well, Ev."

"Goodnight, darling."

She's going to be my ruin.

I've come to the conclusion that she will be my undoing. My mind, body, and soul; It's all hers.

Staring at her now, I can't imagine why she thinks that she's anything less than perfect. Who told her those things? Who belittled her so much that she sees herself as a waste of space?

I refuse to let her think that.

Even if it takes me until the day I die, I will make sure that Evelyn knows that she's the most beautiful person on this planet.

~~~

HEYYYYYYYYYYYYYYYYSo there's some bad blood between Michael and Derek, but why? All will be revealed in time. I hate Derek already though hahaI'm an independent person who can and will stand up for myself, but Michael being protective is kind of hot. He can defend my honor any dayNow Michael knows how Evelyn feels about herself? How ever will that conversation go?Next chapter we're back in Evelyn's POV. It's been fun with Michael, but I'm ready for Evelyn's funny inner thoughts again.See you all soon!
~~~

Chapter 11 - Wowwwwwww

Chapter Song: Photograph by Cody Fry

EvelynI woke up to the smell of mint and the feeling of warm arms wrapped around me.

I slowly peeled my eyes open, adjusting to the light.

Michael was laying with his arms around me, deep asleep.

I can see his freckles so much clearer now than that time at the beach. I didn't realize he had so many then. It's like a star struck him in the face and left the most beautiful marks behind.

I thought I had freckles once, turns out my pores were just clogged.

Anyway.

His hair looks soft and I just want to study his face for hours: The curve of his nose, the slight curl of his eyelashes, the freckles dusted across his cheeks.

All of it. I want to study all of it.

I want to make him smile too. I've seen him half smile before, yes, but never a full, broad smile. I want to see if he has dimples or not. I want to see if his head tilts back when he laughs or if he doubles over instead.

It's just hit me that I might accidentally get Michael sick. He's been with me since, I don't even know how long.

I tried to turn around and look for a clock, but Michael's arms tightened around me, silently urging me to stay.

I want to stay, I really do, but I'd feel bad if I gave him a fever too.

I tried to move again and he grumbled into my hair, "Stop moving. Go back to sleep."

"I don't want to get you sick," I whispered, wiggling out of his grasp. "You go back to sleep and I'll get up."

"You're not going to drop this, are you?" Michael sighed, defeated.

"You know me better than that, darling."

Huh.

Darling.

That was unexpected...I like it.

But what if he doesn't like it? He could hate the nickname, for all I know. I already call him Batman excessively, and he doesn't seem like he minds, but who knows.

I guess the nickname thing between the two of us isn't unusual. For him, it's Batman and darling, For me it's Ev and (maybe?) sweetheart. I feel like he's called me sweetheart, but, truthfully, I don't remember if what I'm thinking of was real or a fever dream.

And I did dream of a shark swimming in sand while chasing a garden gnome in a desert, so the fever dream option is entirely plausible.

I chance a glance at Michael because he's been silent. He's not saying a single thing and now I'm regretting even saying anything at all-

But he it seems he doesn't need to. He's staring at me with an expression that resembles the feeling of breathlessness.

And he's wearing the shadow of a smile.

"What is it?"

"Nothing. Do you want something to eat?"

I want to push it, I really do, but now that he's said it I'm starving.

"Yeah, let's do it."

~~~

"I have bread."

"Do you mean toast?"

"No, Bread. My toaster broke. I have," Michael checked his fridge and pantry again. "Nothing. Nothing but bread, cheese, and three apples."

Michael sighed and threw a piece of bread onto a pan over the stove. I couldn't help my laugh. "Michael, why haven't you been to the market?"

"I was going to go Tuesday afternoon, but there was an...unexpe cted turn of events."

I looked down, maybe taking his joke a little bit too personally, "Sorry."
~~~

"Hey," I heard Michael say. He gently outstretched his hand and tilted my chin up to meet his gaze. "You did nothing wrong."

But I felt wasn't worried. It shifted into something else.

I was distracted.

Distracted by the feel of his hand on my chin, my skin suddenly burning from his touch.

I waited for him to move, but was rooted to the ground as if it were a lifeline. There was something in his eyes that I'm sure matched mine. His mouth parted and his gaze fell from my eyes to my lips.

Oh God.

Is this about to happen?

He suddenly looked me in the eyes and I don't think I'll be able to breath for the next month. "Can I-"

"Yes," I breathed.

Slowly, oh so slowly, he leaned in to me, just a hair of space between us...

Beep beep beep went the smoke detector.

We pulled away (end my life right now) and looked around, just now noticing the smoke.

"Shit! The bread," Michael turned around and turned the heat off of the stove while I opened his window and fanned the smoke out of the room.

The beeping stopped and I couldn't help but laugh.

Michael, who, moments ago, was the picture of desire, now holds part of a dismantled smoke detector and looks completely disheveled and mildly flustered.

"How about we go to my apartment for breakfast?" I suggested, teasingly.

"Yeah, I guess so." Michael grumbled.

I started to turn around to get my shoes, then I remembered.

"Oh shit!" I yelled.

"What is it? What's wrong?"

"Wasabi! I haven't been home so he hasn't eaten!"

~~~

Update: Wasabi isn't dead.

Michael said that he fed Wasabi before he took me to his apartment, so it hasn't been a full forty eight hours since Wasabi's eaten.

"Wait a minute, how did you know how much to feed him?"

"I googled it," Michael shrugged. He said it in a way that made it seem like it wasn't the sweetest thing that he googled fish care just so Wasabi wouldn't die.

It felt so...domestic. Almost as if this is something normal, a routine we follow every day. I felt like the puzzle pieces were being put back together again. And maybe, just maybe, this could be something.

~~~

HEYYYYYYYYYYYYAwwww they really like each otherSorry for the late chapter and if this is moderate trash, it's been a weekAnywayyyyyyyy you're comments on the chapters a few days ago had me cackling, thank you. See y'all soon!

Chapter 12 - Killer Instincts

Chapter Song: Never Gonna Give You Up by Rick Astley (Because that's the closest I can get to rickrolling you guys on the day where it is expected to rickroll everyone you know: April Fools Day)

EvelynI think if people in horror movies possessed more than two brain cells, they'd live to the end of the movie.

If the killer is standing in the kitchen behind the stairs, don't run up the stairs. Turn around and run out the door. If the door won't open for whatever bizarre reason, then run up the stairs, lock a door, and jump out of the window and run.

Honestly, it's not that hard.

But what should also be taken into consideration is the adrenaline and fear of having an axe Murder break into your house and the fear makes you not think irrationally.

But still.

Just run. It's like in Zombieland. Rule #1: Cardio.

I say all of this like I wouldn't be one of the idiots hiding in a pantry from a murderer. But I truly don't think it'd be me.

I've seen enough horror movies to know how not to die in the first five minutes of the movie.

So, I'm good. However, I don't know if Michael is as versed in horror movie survive skills as me.

~~~

I texted him to meet me in my apartment today.

Now, in a completely non stalker way, I'm watching him from behind a plant just outside the door of my apartment.

He knocks on the door.

Me: HeyMe: The door is unlocked, you can come in.Michael : Okay

I watched Michael reach for the doorknob and pull on it, the knob coming off in his hands.

"Shit," I heard him mutter.

He looked side to side and I caught a glimpse of his face. His eyes were wide and he looked a little bit worried.

Once he deadpanned at the door knob I couldn't contain my laughter.

Michael whipped around, frazzled to see me laughing on the staircase.

"What..."

"The doorknob," I started in between wheezing breaths, walking towards him, "It falls off all the time."
~~~

Michael had a hint of a smile that he was trying his best to hide. "You...pranked me?"

I put my hand on his shoulder, "Happy April Fools Day."

"You got me."

"That I did, darling." I replied, satisfied beyond words.

"I did bring this for you," he held up a plastic bag, "Kind of as an 'I'm glad you're feeling better present,' but now I'm reconsidering."

"Michael, I am truly sorry for scaring you, but it is April Fools, it's what the day entails."

"Fine," Michael grumbled. "You can have it."

I squealed and grabbed the bag. There was a box of candy inside.

"Michael," I started, opening the box, "Thank you so much-"

I shrieked when something jumped out of the box and hit me.

Then proceeded to throw the box at Michael. In self defense. Well, mine, not his.

I was breathing heavily, looking at him with wild eyes, and he laughed.

He threw his head back, eyes closed and dimples showing, and started laughing so hard I thought he would run out of air.

I think I would have enjoyed the moment more if an unknown object hadn't just hit me.

I looked down to see a hard plastic snake on the floor. It was a trick box.

Oh my God.

He pranked me.

Michael fucking Laurent just scared the shit out of me.

I picked up the snake on the ground and threw it at him. "That was not funny! You have me a fucking heart attack!"

But he kept laughing.

If I'm being honest, the joke was hilarious. He really did get me. But, right now, I'm running half on shock and adrenaline and the other half on triple shot espresso.

"I'm going to get you back for that," I stated simply.

I already have a plan. He'll just have to wait until tomorrow to see it unfold.

"I look forward to it," Michael says, wiping tears from his eyes.

"I really should've thought about this plan more. Now that the doorknob's broken, I can't get into my apartment."

Michael stopped suddenly, realizing the logic in my words. "Not another prank?"

"No, we'll just have to push the door open now."

~~~

"Coffee for Michael," I call the order, smiling smugly in my head.

Michael always orders black coffee every morning, I thought I'd switch it up for him today.

Today he is going to be drinking a Cinnamon Dulce de Leche Latte.

That's (off the record) Clairo's ripoff of the Starbucks drink 'Cinnamon Dolce Latte.' I don't know how, probably the black market, now that I think about it, but Clairo herself found the exact recipe for the drink and now we've ripped it off.
~~~

Michael should have some sugar in his system so he can approach the day with joy instead of glaring at everyone. Like he is now.

"Thanks," Michael says with a warm, shy smile as he walks up to me and takes the drink.

"You're welcome," I chirp.

Michael walked out and now all that's left is for me to wait.

~~~

Sure enough, when I got off of work I saw a text from Michael.

Michael : Ev, you're amazing, but I think you gave me the wrong drinkMe: No, I didn'tMichael : It wasn't black coffeeMe: I knowMichael : It was sweetMe: Once again, I knowMichael : So you intentionally gave me that sugary monstrosityMe: It is not a monstrosityMe: You need more joy in your life, sugar is a good place to startMichael : I have joy in my lifeMe: Doing what? Terrorizing the citizens of California?Michael : YesMe: I knew itMe: and I bet you liked the drinkMichael : ...Michael : NoMe: So that's a yes thenMichael : ...Me: If you want, I'll make you another one tomorrowMichael : NoMe: Are you sure?Me: You hesitatedMe: That's twice nowMichael : FineMichael : But I still don't like itMe: Uh huh, keep telling yourself thatMe: I knew you'd love itMe: I'll put in extra cinnamon tomorrow, just for youMe: I'm going to stop texting you before you change your mindMe: ByeeeeeeeeeeeeeeMichael : Bye Ev

~~~

HEYYYYYYYYYYYYYYYYHappy April Fool's Day all!!!My friend pranked me today and it kind of set the tone for the rest of the day. I'm really craving cosido right now and I just can't get the thought out of my head. If you don't know what cosido is you're missing out, it's delicious. If there are typos, I'll fix them later. In complete honesty, I'm too tired to reread and spellcheck this, sorry If anyone is still awake right now, try and go to sleep if you can.Take care of yourselves. You matter <3

Chapter 13 - Convenient Coincidences

Chapter Song: Bad Feeling by Cobra Man

EvelynMichael has come into Clairo's every day this week and ordered the 'sugary monstrosity.'

I knew he would like it, and I'm, quite frankly, disappointed in his lack of faith in me. I find it disturbing.

(Sorry, I couldn't help the Star Wars reference.)

But then again, that's just the day.

I always, always, sleep in on Saturday mornings, but today I couldn't. I don't know why. Was it my date with Michael tomorrow? Maybe I'm just nervous.

Michael's planned the last three dates we've gone on, and they've all been amazing. The problem with that is now I'm planning one and I'm scared he won't like it.

Honestly, how do people plan a perfectly heartwarming and fun date and not have an anxiety attack over whether it's good enough or not?

I know what Michael likes and dislikes, so that helps me a lot.

Likes: The color gold, sit coms, movies, pasta, Queen, and scented candles.

Dislikes: Spicy food, Hawaiian pizza, apple sauce, crayons, people who walk slow, people who drive slow, people who don't use their turn signals on their cars, people who...well, exist.

People. He dislikes people.

It's easiest to find out what to do based off of what someone doesn't like and then work from there.

Doesn't like people? Somewhere private then.

Likes pasta? I can make a good bowl of spaghetti.

Movies? What pasta themed movies-

Oh my God. I got it.

I can set up a cute little picnic on the floor of my apartment, make spaghetti, and we can watch Lady and the Tramp.

It's perfect. It'll be cold, so the weather suits the occasion well. Some good comfort food and I have some great company in Michael.

With this sudden wave of inspiration, I feed Wasabi and get the plan in motion.

~~~

I'm halfway through a rather bland bagel when there's a knock at my door.
~~~

I instantly pause, wearily looking at the door. Michael's at work and I didn't order anything off of Amazon, so there shouldn't be anyone at the door.

I walk to the door and grab the baseball bat I keep by my front door, just in case. Since there's no peephole on the door, I never know who's outside. It's always better to be safe then sorry, especially in this shitty apartment.

Slowly, I open the door.

There's something familiar about the man standing in front of me. He's maybe twenty six years old and he has grey eyes. The grey could only be described as a an all consuming storm that ravages everything in its path.

"Hello, Evelyn," the stranger says politely, all smooth voice and steady eye contact.

"Hi," I respond slowly, tightening my grip on the bat behind my back. "How do you know my name?"

"I'm so sorry. How rude of me to not introduce myself. I'm Derek, Michael's brother."

And it all made sense. That's why he, Derek, looks so familiar. Him and Michael have almost the same hair color, Derek's being a little bit lighter than Michael's, and the exact same sharp jawline. They looked similar enough to be able to tell that they're bothers, but not so similar that one would think they were twins.

Although Derek gave me a warm smile, there was something behind his eyes, something secretive. Almost as if he was plotting some elaborate scheme that will leave everyone speechless.

But then again, I've only talked to him for thirty seconds.

"Hi!" I greeted back, cheerfully disguising any worry or judgment that could've come through my tone. "I didn't know that you lived around here. Did you buy the space upstairs?"

"No, I was just coming to visit. I saw Michael last week and he mentioned that he didn't have time to talk since someone he really cares about wasn't feeling well."

Aw, he 'really cares' about me? And he's not shamed to tell people?

"He mentioned your name," Derek continued, "and it stuck with me because of the way he said it. I've never seen him like that before, it was nice."

Maybe the feeling I got earlier was wrong, I was probably unjustifiably judging the day, and Derek, based off of nothing but a bad nights sleep.

I can confidently say this for a fact because the guy in front of me does not sound like a conniving axe murderer.

He still could be, but he doesn't give off the vibe.

"And I'm not a stalker, I promise. I didn't pull a Joe Goldberg on you. I just got lucky when I walked by downstairs and heard these two sweet old ladies talking about their 'angel of a neighbor, Evelyn.' With the way Michael talked about you, I had a feeling I had the right Evelyn."

I was honestly too stunned to speak. I don't know what knocked my breath away more: What Michael said about me or how well spoken Derek was.

Taking in a shocked expression, Derek added, "I decided to see where you lived because I wanted to thank you. It looks like you've helped my brother and I appreciate it."

"I didn't even know I was helping," I responded. It was all I could think of to say.

"That's the best part."

We stood there for a moment, kind of awkward, and I felt so rude for having him just stand in the doorway. "Do you want to come in for a moment? I feel bad that you're standing there after all the trouble you went through to come up here."

"No, I should go. But you're kindness is noted and appreciated. Goodbye, Evelyn."

He turned to go, but stopped mid step, a movement I couldn't help but notice that Michael does too.

"Oh," Derek turned around to face me, a sneaky smoky splayed across his face, "Happy almost birthday. It's going to be a blast to turn twenty one."

Derek pivoted on his heel and walked away, whistling a tune that sent shivers down to my core.

How the hell does he know when my birthday is?

~~~

HEYYYYYYYYYYYYYYYYThree updates, three days in a row, I think I'm on a rollAnd what is Derek doing at Evelyn's apartment? Do we really buy his story with an awful lot of convenient coincidences? HmmmmmmmmmmmAnd what will Michael do when he
~~~

finds out?So many questions, and no answers yet. Sorry for thatOkay, I'm out for the evening. Byeeeee

Chapter 14 - I Hate Clocks

Chapter Songs (There are two because I couldn't decide): An Empty Cup (And a Broken Date) by Roy Orbison and Break my Heart Again by FINNEAS

EvelynI'd like to say that I'm not a judgy person, but Derek gave off ace murderer vibes.

How in the absolute hell did he know when my birthday is? That's so creepy. Unless he googled me, which, I guess, is still creepy. Maybe he googled me with good intentions?

I think I'll call Michael and tell him about it after he gets off of work, maybe he knows something I don't and I just want to steer on the side of caution.

What was I going to do before Mr. Creepy Guy Derek knocked on my door?

Oh right. Grocery shopping.

~~~

I think grocery stores would be even better if they sold little individual cakes for one. I don't need a whole cake or anything, and a slice
~~~

feels too aggressive, I just want a cute little cake that I can eat and be depressed or happy with.

I also think grocery stores would be better if they found a way to have mangoes year round. If I wasn't broke and could eat a mango every day, I would.

I guess since I'm already pitching ideas to the grocery stores then why not have every grocery store set up like Sam's Club or Costco and give out free samples?

Want to try this brand of pesto sauce? Free sample. Want to try this guacamole? Free sample. Want to try this pumpkin pie? Free sample.

Everyone in the world would be happier if this was a thing.

Even right now, I need to choose between three brands of spaghetti sauce that all have the exact same ingredients in it. I just don't get it. Which one is best? Which one is worst?

I would know the answer if I could try a free sample.

"Evelyn?"

I turn around, surprised to hear my name in the pasta sauce aisle of a grocery store, and see Derek standing behind me.

"Derek? Hi."

"Hi, this is a weird coincidence."

Yeah, really really really weird.

"Yeah, what are you doing here?"

Buying groceries you idiot. Or stalking me.

"I'm buying peanut butter and steak," Derek held up the jar of peanut butter he had in his hand, "It's my dog's birthday tomorrow so I'm giving her peanut butter in the morning and steak for dinner. Lean steak though, I don't want her to get sick."

"That's really sweet," I say, truthful. "Happy early birthday to her."

"Thanks. I was walking to get the steak from the fridge at the end of the isle when I saw you here. I thought I'd say hi."

"Thank you, then." I pause, gathering my courage. "One quick question, how do you know when my birthday is?"

Derek winced, "I'm so sorry, I realize I might have come off on the creepy side. Truthfully, I looked you up online."

I knew it.

"It's just," Derek continued, "Michael's had his heart broken in the past, and it left him wrecked. I just wanted to make sure that you were a good person. Which, I think that you are. I wanted to do for him what I know he would've done for me."

Okay, maybe I was wrong. That was such a genuine answer that now I feel bad of accusing him of having axe murderer vibes.

"I think it's really nice if you to care for him that much. And no worries, I was only a little bit freaked out," I chuckled.

Derek laughed too, "Yeah, sorry again. I've been told I give off that impression. I think it's my eyes. I kind of a creepy eyes."

"We all have our things, it's no worry. And now that I've established that you're not going to stab me with a kitchen knife, it's very nice to meet you."

"You too. And would you please do me a favor and not tell Michael about us meeting? I was only supposed to be in town for a few days for work but I asked to stay longer so I could visit him. I want to surprise him tomorrow night."

"I won't say a thing then. And tomorrow night Michael and I will be out on a date, so he won't be at his apartment."

"Oh?"

"Yeah," I gesture to the endless rows of pasta sauce in front of me. "I'm trying to pick which pasta sauce to get."

Derek looked at all of the sauces and grabbed one from the back. "Get this one. Our mom used to make this one for us when we were younger. He'll like it."

"Thank you," I say sincerely. Wow, I really was wrong about him.

"I should get going. You have a good evening, Evelyn."

"Thank you, you too. Tell your dog I say happy birthday."

Derek smiled at me again, warm and appreciative, "Thank you, I will."

~~~

Everything is ready for mine and Michael's date now.

I spent the last two hours building the most intricate pillow fort on the planet and I couldn't be prouder.

I have soft music playing to create a nice vibe in the room. I even have the food ready for cooking on the counter so we can cook together. Even luckier for me, my apartment isn't freezing cold or boiling hot. It's just right. Everything is just right.

Next on the list of things to do before Michael gets here is to check my hair in the mirror. I have it in French braids and for once there aren't a bunch of small strands poking out of the braid. I told him
~~~

the attire was casual, like 'wear your pjs or else' causal. So I'm wearing my superhero themed sweatpants and a t-shirt.

I check the time and it's seven fifty five. Michael said he'd be over at 8.

And all that left to do is wait.

And wait.

And wait.

I call him at half past eight to see where he is. He doesn't call me back.

I watch as the hands on the clock move while I stay frozen in place, watching a door that hasn't opened.

I call him again at ten. I hope for a response, I don't get one.

With each tick of the clock I feel like I'm being laughed at, mocked for being so naive that I thought he wouldn't be like the rest.

Even though it's midnight, I can help but sit facing the door and hearing the endless tick, tick, tick.

~~~

HEYYYYYYYYYYYYYYYYYYYYYYFirst of all, sorry for that. I felt the pain writing it. Poor Evelyn. Michael stood up Evelyn. He better have a good reason or I'm gonna smack him.And what's up with the sudden change with Derek? What ever could he be planning. I definitely don't know anything about it...If anyone has school and/or work this week, good luck! You've got this!Also, if anyone has something or nothing to do this week, you've got this. You rock. Thanks for 3k views! I appreciate it!
~~~

Chapter 15 - Groveling Only Gets You So Far

Chapter Song: Falling by Harry Styles

MichaelI had the weirdest dream last night.

Evelyn came to my apartment and kept knocking on my door over and over again asking if I was alright. I told her-

Shit.

Shit shit shit shit shit.

Evelyn.

I was supposed to see her last night.

I unplug my phone and unmute it: 5 missed calls and 9 messages.

No no no...

8:20 p.m.Ev : HeyEv : Are you still coming over?

9:00 p.m.Ev : Can you please text me back or return my calls so I k now you're okay?

9:15 p.m.Ev : Michael?

10:45 p.m.Ev : Either you just stood me up or something is really wrongEv : And seeing as how you don't seem like the kind of guy to stood me up then I'm thinking that something is wrong

12:08 p.m.Ev : I was wrongEv : Don't call me back. I won't respond

No. This can't be happening. How was I so stupid to forget that our date was last night. She seemed so excited to, it's all she talked about all week.

I'm a terrible person. I hope she forgives me. I don't know if I would've forgiven me, though. I certainly don't deserve it. But I have to try.

I need to talk to her. I will grovel for her her attention alone if I have to. I need to make this right. She doesn't deserve to be treated that shitty.

I text her back but she doesn't answer. I even try and call her.

She stayed true to her word.

~~~

I open the door to Clairo's and see Evelyn instantly. Even in a crowd of thousands of people I would be able to find her instantly.

But she looks different today.

That glow she always carries around herself and the slight bounce in her step is nowhere to be seen. She hasn't turned around to see that it's me in the doorway yet. But when she does, I'm afraid to see the look on her face.

"Hi," Evelyn starts, greeting me with a cheery voice that was so convincing I almost believed it was real. "What can I-"
~~~

Her smile falls when she turns around and sees me. I fear I might drop to my knees in front of everyone and beg for her not to look at me like she is now, eyes full of sadness, betrayal, and anger.

"Ev," I start, unsure of what to say to make things better. "I'm so sor-"

"Do you want your usual?"

What? Why is she asking-

Oh.

That's not good.

"Ev-"

"Michael, I'm really busy right now and I don't have time for this."

"Okay," I say, softly. I need to make this right. "Yeah, I'll have my usual."

She turns around silently and makes my coffee. It doesn't take her as long as usual to make it today.

Maybe she's just rushing.

"You know the total."

Ouch.

I ignore the song in my chest at her sudden coldness and hand her the money. With her no longer looking at me, I take a moment to study her face. She used makeup to hide the evidence of a bad nights sleep and the pain that I caused her. Her face is void of any and all emotion and it's scaring me. She's completely closed herself off to me.

What's killing me, though, is I don't know what she's thinking. Ev doesn't even look at me when she wordlessly hands me my coffee.

"Ev, can we talk? Please?" I beg. I beg for a sign of anything. Just something to show that she still may care and that I didn't screw things up forever.

When Evelyn looks at me, her eyes are filled with rage. "You want to talk? After what you said to me last night do you really think that I'll sit around and listen to you talk?"

What did I say last night? I don't remember seeing her, much less talking to her.

"I'm so sorry, I-"

"Michael. I need to get back to doing my job. We can talk later."

I can't argue with her. Not after what I did and, apparently, what I said. I've treated her like shit, the least I could do is stop bothering her.

"Okay. I'll talk to you later," I offer her a half smile before walking outside and sitting by the bench outside of the cafe. I'll wait here until her shift is done.

I take a sip of my coffee and am instantly taken aback.

It's black coffee.

She hasn't given me black coffee in over a week. She's been giving me that sugary shit every day because she knows I love it.

But today it's just plain, boring black coffee.

Shit.

~~~

When Evelyn sees me on the bench she turns around and walks the other way.

"Ev, please, listen to me."
~~~

"No," She bit back, furious. "You stood me up, you listen to me." Ev took a deep breath, trying to calm herself down. "I waited for you. All night."

"I know."

"No, you don't. I waited and waited for a text or a phone call that never came. And I thought," she laughed humorlessly, "I thought you were in trouble. That maybe something bad happened to you because you weren't at my apartment and I knew that you weren't the type to just bail on me without a word. Then I show up to your apartment, after hours of worry, and knock on the door. Do you remember what you said to me?"

"No," I reply with the answer that killed me to know would hurt her more.

"Figures. You told me: 'Go the fuck away. I don't want you here if you're going to continue to be that fucking annoying.'"

Oh no. Ev...

"Tell me right now and tell me honestly," Evelyn says, tears sliding down her cheeks, "Did you have a good reason to not show up last night?"

"No."

"Why didn't you come?"

I couldn't meet her eyes. I couldn't see what I did to her.

"Michael. Why didn't you come?"

"I forgot," I whispered.

I dare a glance at her face and regretted it instantly. Her face has fallen completely and she looks like she's about to break down and cry on sidewalk.

"You forgot about us? About me?" Her voice was barely above a whisper.

"Yes," I bow my head in shame. "I'm so sorry."

Now it's Evelyn's turn to not be able to maintain eye contact. She looks to the sky and closes her eyes. It takes me only a moment to realize that she's crying. I know that I hurt her, but I feel like I hurt her in a way I don't even know about.

I want so desperately to reach my hand out, to pull her into my arms and give her a safe space to just cry.

But I can't.

Her tears are my fault. It's all my fault.

"I can't do this right now," She whispers between shaky breaths. "I can't. I'll text you when I'm ready to talk but I- I can't right now."

Next thing I know, I feel tears begin to fall down my own cheeks as I watch her walk away.

~~~

HEYYYYYYYYYYYYYYYYYBefore I say anything, I'm so so so sorry.That whole chapter was nothing but pain.Oops. (Please don't hurt me)Things will get bette for the two of them in the next chapter or two, depends on how I want to go with it on the emotional damage scale hahaOnce more, please don't hurt meI love you all <3Byeeeeeeeeeeeeeeeee
~~~

Chapter 16 - Untold Stories

Chapter Song: All I Ask of You by Original Cast of Phantom of the Opera

MichaelI hate myself for making her cry. I sat in my car for far too long, unable to move or speak.

How could I have forgotten our date?

I'd never leave her waiting.

I was really tired after work last night so I took a nap. But my shift ended at 4, there's no way I slept for 16 hours.

This is stupid. This is all so fucking stupid.

That hurt in her eyes, it was so deep that I know I touched a wound that hasn't healed. I might've just ruined everything.

~~~

What the fuck.

"Michael, it's so good to see you again."
~~~

Fucking Derek is leaning on the doorframe of my apartment like he owns it. What the fuck is up with him leaning against doorways?

"The hell are you doing here?" I ask, shoving past him to unlock my apartment door and slam it in his face.

"I just wanted to know how your date with Evelyn went last night."

I stopped moving completely. How did he know about that? He would've had to have been stalking-

No. He could've just had a lucky guess and is trying to piss me off. He's a liar but not worth my time.

"You think you're smart?" I say pulling out my key to unlock my door, "We didn't have a date last night. Nice try."

Derek snapped his fingers and smacked himself on the forehead. "Right, that's my bad, I forgot you bailed on her."

I stopped moving once more.

That little shit.

"You really should invest in an alarm, you probably wouldn't have slept through your date if you had one."

I slowly looked up at him and glared, a silent warning for him to stop talking. He may be older than me, but I'm stronger than him.

"Then again, maybe if you payed closer attention to the water bottle you always leave out in the open you would've seen someone slip something inside-"

All I could hear was my heart pounding in my chest as I dropped my keys and shoved him into the wall. "What did you do?"

Derek put his hands up in a mocking display of innocence. "Nothing you can prove."

"Did you drug me?"

"Why would I do that? You're my brother and I love you. Besides, that's illegal."

"Uh huh. Don't act like you have done illegal shit before."

"You should deal with your trust issues, Michael. It's not a healthy habit."

I let him go, pushing him away from me. "Stay away from Evelyn and I. If I see you again so help me I'll call your parole officer."

"A good talk as always. See you later."

What did I just say?

~~~

Evelyn texted me at 5:30 that evening.

Ev : Hey. Can we talk?Me: YesMe: PleaseMe: When?Ev : 7 at my a partmentEv : If you want

If you want to show up is what she meant.

Me: YesMe: I'll be there

~~~

I was outside of her apartment at 6:30.

I paced until exactly 7 o'clock when I knocked.

Evelyn opened the door instantly, almost if she was as anxious to have this conversation as I was.

"Come in," was all she said.

I wiped my hands on jeans, suddenly even more nervous than before.

She sat leaning against the headboard of her bed, holding a pillow to her chest. I sat on the very edge of her bed, waiting for her to speak.

"First, I want to say that I forgive you," She pauses.

What?

"No, no. I'm sorry."

"I know. And, honestly, you should be. What you said hurt, but I know you didn't mean it."

"How are you forgiving me? I was an asshole."

"Yeah, but it was an honest mistake. I can't fault you for being human. And I could hear it in your voice, I woke you up." She smiled to herself, "You always drawl your words when you're tired, and you did it last night."

I don't know what to say.

"I knew you didn't mean what you said yet I was cruel to you anyway."

"No, you weren't-

"Yes, I was. And I'm sorry. But you deserve to know why I reacted as I did." Evelyn drew in a shaking breath, holding her pillow tighter, "When I was younger, it was just my dad and I. But he didn't like me. He said it was my fault she died. One time he promised me that he'd take me to a skate park. He drove me there, told me forgot something at home, and drove away. I waited for him for eight hours before my friend's mom saw me alone and drove me home."

A tear slipped down her cheek, "It's been almost eleven years since that day, but I've never forgotten that feeling. That sinking, dreadful feeling of realizing that no one is coming. Or, even worse, that no one cares enough to come. I hadn't felt it since he died but, I felt it last night. When you didn't show up I felt just like I was that little girl at the skate park again."

Whatever showed on my face, empathy, pain, she looked at me with a sad smile. "I'm okay now, Michael. It was a long time ago. Honestly, I haven't thought about that day in years, but...I thought about it all of last night and this morning. I know you didn't mean to, but you struck a nerve in me. I just wanted you to know why I acted how I did."

I opened my mouth to say something, but she held up her hand, silencing me.

"I'm not done. I'm still hurt that you forgot. Despite whatever happened for you to forget the date, you stood me up. And that's not okay."

I sighed, "I'm sorry, Ev. You deserve to know why and quite honestly it's a pathetic excuse but I was so tired after work I just wanted to take a nap, I didn't mean to sleep the whole evening."

"Michael, that's fine. But if you felt like shit before coming, just tell me and reschedule. It's no big deal. Communicate, Michael. It helps both sides."

"Okay, I will. I promise. I'll communicate everything."

"Everything?"

"Yes, I'll never shut up."

"You? I highly doubt it," She laughed and everything felt right again.

~~~
~~~

HEYYYYYYYYYYYYYIf that was trash, sorry, I wrote this at 4 a.m. and writing them making up was a lot more difficult than expected And YAY they're back and happy together. Whatever could Derek have been (allegedly) doing? HmmmmmmI'm going to try and put out another chapter later today or tomorrow. Bye!!!

Chapter 17 - Finally

Chapter Song: I Hear a Symphony by Cody Fry

EvelynIf I was told I could have any practical superpower, it would be to eat whatever I want and not gain weight. Honestly, eating carbs every day of my life without consequence sounds like a very good deal.

The first thing I do when I walk into a restaurant is look to see if there is complimentary bread on the tables.

If I had the patience and will to work out every day, I would eat bread and pasta every day. But I don't.

Now that it's the middle of summer, it is hot.

California somehow always gets that dead heat that makes one want to move to Alaska just for a break from the heat.

When I saw that today's high was 103 degrees, I debated booking a flight to Alaska myself. The heat was so intolerable that I woke up in my oven of an apartment at 6 am.

But Michael texted me around 7.

Michael : HeyMichael : Do you want to go to the beach today?Me: Fuck yesMe: It's too hot todayMichael : CoolMichael : We'll, not really, but you know what I meanMichael : I'll pick you up at 8?Me: Sounds like a plan Batman

I could practically see him shaking his head at his phone.

Things have been good between us, better even. It feels almost as if there's an unspoken deeper understanding between the two of us. I think we have something special. I don't know why, I just have a feeling.

~~~

Shit.

I have to wear a bikini.

I'm broke and lazy so the only bathing suit I own is a bikini I bought two years ago.

What if I don't look good in it? What if I've gained weight and now the bikini makes me look fat. Dear Lord, I was not expecting a mental breakdown this morning.

It's a cute bikini though. It's midnight blue with a sparkle woven into the top that makes it look like stars.

But what if he doesn't think I look good? However irrational it may sound, what if this is an automatic turn off for him and he decides that I'm not worth it?

I'll deal with that later. For now, I need to finish getting ready because Michael will be here any minute and I haven't eaten or put something on or-

Knock knock knock.
~~~

Shit. Okay.

"One second!"

I run to my closet and grab a sundress to go over my bikini and I put on my sandals. I may have used a little too much strength to open my front door because it flew open. I stumbled back a step to account for the kick back.

Michael was staring at me with wide eyes, shock and confusion blending into quite possibly the funniest expression he's worn. In all honesty, he looked like a startled puppy.

"Stupid bipolar door," I muttered under my breath.

Michael chuckled, beyond amused at my struggle.

"This isn't funny," I pointed at him. "I don't need you making fun of my broken door. It's been through enough."

"I have no intention of doing that. I am simply observing a not funny at all situation."

I narrowed my eyes at him, unconvinced. Michael smiled and gave me a thumbs up. I couldn't help laughing as I walked past him and closed the door. "Oh shut up. I'm getting in the car now."

~~~

There are a lot of things in life that make me want to lock myself in my room for the rest of eternity: The beach is not one of them.

There's something about the smell of salt water and the feeling of waves rolling over my feet that's so freeing. The light breeze and warm sunlight caresses my skin and I can breathe.

Just being here, with Michael who-

Who is staring at me.
~~~

"Is everything alright?" I ask slowly.

"Yes," Michael smiles fondly, "Everything is more than alright."

"Good, because I'm going to race you to the water."

I take off running across the sand, Michael following closely.

"Shit!" I yell, laughing. "The sand so hot. Why is it so fucking hot?"

Ever the athlete, Michael surpasses me in a matter of seconds and is bolting towards the water. He may be faster, but...

No but. He's just faster.

"Did you," I panted once I reached the water, "Did you do track in high school or something? You're fast."

Michael chuckled, "Cross country, actually. And street hockey."

"Street hockey? Okay, Mr. I-posses-a-million-hidden-abilities-that-I've-been-hiding-until-now."

"I can't give away all of secrets."

"Uh huh. I didn't take you as the team sports type. You're too broody."

"Yes, me and my life of solitary darkness. I spread misery everywhere I go," Michael sarcastically quipped.

"Exactly," I responded with a smile. "You're all doom and gloom."

Michael looked at my with a devilish grin.

I narrowed my eyes at him, "Michael, whatever you're going to do-"

Before I knew it he kicked a shit ton of water directly at me.

"Oops."

"Michael!" I shrieked backing up a few steps. He laughed and did it again. "That's freezing!"

But he kept smiling and chased me.

"Hold on, hold on," I said in between running from him. "Let's think logically. How about we put our stuff down and then I can push you into the water without worrying about breaking your phone. Or mine."

Michael stopped his approach for a moment before looking at me. "One minute. And challenge accepted."

We both ran out of the water and threw off our clothes, tucking our phones in our shirts so they don't overheat. I looked at Michael and-

"Holy shit," I whispered. He has muscles. I knew that before, but, I can actually see them now. He's not ripped, but he's muscular enough for me to stop thinking for a second.

"See something you like?" Michael asked, blushing behind his smirk.

"No."

"You're blushing."

"As are you." He blushed a little bit harder but his stare intensified, never breaking eye contact with me.

"It's hot, shut up," I grumbled, feeling my face heat up some more."

"Come on, the minute is over. And I believe that you promised me you'd attempt to tackle me."

"Attempt? Okay, hockey star, prepare to have your dreams of escape absolutely crushed."

I ran to the water and Michael followed suit.

I immediately turned around and kicked a lot of water at him. He backed up a step, blinking a lot. "You got water in my eye."

"Sorry, I didn't-"

Michael ran forward and grabbed me, picking me up bridal style and running deeper into the water.

"Michael, put me down!" I laughed.

He didn't; He kept running until he was just over waist deep in the water and I was crying laughing at him to stop or I'd drown. Gently, he put me down. The water went up to just below my chest and I looked up at him, smiling in awe.

Up this close I could see everything again, just like that day in his apartment. But now I get to see him in the daytime.

And at my favorite place.

Sand was littered in his hair and his eyes seemed even greener against the blue water.

"You're beautiful," he said.

"Me? No, you're the one who's beautiful."

"Thank you, but don't deflect. Ev, you're the most beautiful person I've ever met," Michael said softly. "You have the kindest heart I've ever known and...you make me believe that there is good in this world. All I need to see is that sparkle in your eyes and I know I'll be okay."

"Michael, that's the nicest thing anyone's said to me."

"It's the truth. And I can't wait another moment before asking you," Michael took a breath. "Evelyn, would you please do me the greatest honor and allow me to be your boyfriend?"

"Yes," I whisper. It's all I can say. I don't have the words to even try and express how I feel after all that he's told me.

"Yes?"

"Yes."

Michael's breathing hitched, looking at my lips, then my eyes. "I'd like to kiss you now."

I heard my heart racing, "What's stopping you?"

"Nothing anymore."

His eyes fluttered closed as his lips met mine, the touch so gentle, so intimate, that I felt the world drown out and suddenly it was just us.

I could taste the salt water on his lips when I kissed him back, melting into his touch. The movies were right, I felt like I was on top of the world. I felt like there were a million fireworks exploding around me but all I cared about was Michael in front of me.

I felt a small smile creep up on me when we pulled apart for a moment, resting our foreheads against each other, not saying a word.

I knew instantly that I was home.

~~~

HEYYYYYYYYYYYYYYYYYYYThey finally kissed. I couldn't prolong it any longer, I needed it to happen. 17 chapters is long enough, right? And this chapter was okey inspired by the random heat wave last Thursday and Friday in California. That was so random. The AC unit at my house decided to die then, so that was fun.If you're watching Moon Knight right now, you'll get this reference:Laters, gators.
~~~

Chapter 18 - A Twenty Year Old Having a Midlife Crisis and A Broken Door

Chapter Song: The Mission Impossible Theme (from any of the movies)

EvelynIn someone's life, there's the anticipation of turning sixteen: Driving, a little more freedom in some places, and the opportunity of employment.

The next milestone is turning eighteen: There's being taken a lot more seriously, seeing rated R movies by yourself, and, the most anxiety inducing elephant in the room, being an adult.

(Honorable mention to turning twenty and saying goodbye to one's teenage years. That one hurt.)

After that is the daunting yet milestone that I'm facing: Turning twenty one. At eighteen, and even twenty, it's easy to fool yourself into thinking that you're still a child. But at twenty one, no ones fooling anyone. Everyone turns into a fully fledged member of society and the struggles of adulthood.

There's alcohol because it's legal, so there's that too.

I don't see myself as a huge drinker or anything, maybe just a shot of tequila here and a glass of wine there.

But who knows.

My birthday is in a week, so I think I'll stop thinking about my entrance into adulthood for a little bit longer.

~~~

I might have a small problem.

My door won't open.

Generally, that's not a big problem, seeing as this happens every day, but now it really won't open. "Come on, come on, come on," I pleaded to the door. Almost as if it was laughing at me, the door creaked in response.

Now I'm pissed.

"Listen here, fucker," I hissed at my door. "If you don't open right now I swear I will remove you from these hinges and watch you burn in a dumpster fire outside."

I violently and continuously pulled at the doorknob and nothing happened.

"Are you alright, dear?"

I whip around to see my neighbor, Mrs. Owens, staring at me in annoyance and judgement, a fake smile on her face.

I fucking hate Mrs. Owens.
~~~

She has the most judgy eyes I've ever seen on a person. She has light brown hair and always wears the most God awful pant suits. Every time I look at her I feel a boiling range arise in me.

"Yes," I reply, my smile equally as fake as hers, "everything is absolutely delightful."

When she walked away, I sighed in defeat. I sat leaning against my shitty door and just stared at the floor. The wood was so distressed and scratched I'm surprised no one has fallen straight through the floor. There were nicks, scratches, nails sticking up in random places, bleach stains, footpr-

Bleach stains. Was someone murdered in here? If someone was, then now this apartment scares me. There's no way I'm living somewhere where someone was murdered. I don't need that bad energy.

If someone was murdered, then someone was incredibly stupid if they decided to get rid of the bloodstains with bleach on hardwood floors. The alleged killer would have to be amateur because the bleach stain is huge.

Oh. That actually makes me feel worse.

But then again, it's been established that I've seen enough horror movies and seen enough crime tv shows to survive. In theory.

The longer I stare at the bleach stain in front of me the more I want to go hide in my apartment. But I can't do that.

I think I'll call my landlord. Maybe she can fix the door.

~~~

Update: She could not fix the door.
~~~

My landlords, Tina, said "That's not opening. I'll call Hector (the maintenance guy) to fix it when he gets back."

"When does he come back?" I asked.

"Two and half weeks."

"Two and a half weeks? All of my clothes are in my apartment! And where am I supposed to stay?"

"That's your problem. I'll call you once it's fixed."

I'm kind of bummed out. I have a bunch of stuff in there I need and-

"Shit!" I yell. Wasabi. Wasabi is all alone in my apartment and he needs to eat. That fish has been with me for the past two years, I refuse to let him die now.

I try the door again, hoping that maybe with my newfound willpower it will open. It didn't.

I face my back against the door and look at the staircase. Surprise surprise, my other neighbor Adam is standing there. He's 17 and he likes to break into people's apartments.

Generally, I discourage that. But maybe it'll work in my favor this time.

"Adam, come here."

Adam pointed at himself in fake innocence. "Yes, you. The only teenage delinquent in the room."

Once he walked over, I continued, "I have a proposition for you. I will give you ten dollars if you break into my apartment, put my fish in his to go carrier, and bring him to me."

"15 dollars."

"I am literally paying you to commit a crime. It's ten dollars."

"Fine."

"Don't steal anything else," I called after him.

Once he ran off it hit me that I really don't have a place to stay. Normally I'd hang out with my friend Alanna, but she's on vacation in Europe for the summer, so my one and only option is no longer an option.

Unless...

No. I couldn't do that to Michael. That's way too long for me to be staying with him. I wouldn't want to bother him and that it defiantly long enough to be a bother.

My phone rang. Ah, speak of the devil.

"Hi, Michael."

"Hey, Ev. Do you want to watch a mov-wait, hold on." I heard muffling on the other end of the line and then Michael's muffled voice mutter "shit" the line went dead.

That was weird.

I called him back and he picked up almost immediately.

"Shit, sorry. I hit my arm and dropped my phone," Michael cursed.

"That's fine, are you okay?" I asked insinuatingly. I could practically hear him hissing in pain on the other end of the line.

"Don't laugh."

"I'll try not to."

"I ran into a wall and hit my funny bone."

"Did you drop your phone because you hit your funny bone or..."

"Yes, Ev, I dropped my phone because I hit my funny bone."

I stifled my laughter, trying not to make a sound.

"Go ahead, say what you're thinking."

"I didn't think you had a funny bone."

There was a moment of silence before Michael spoke, "I didn't think I had one either."

I couldn't help it. I started laughing. I honestly couldn't tell what I found funnier: my comment or Michael's reaction.

"Anyway," Michael started once I'd calmed down. "You said you have something to show me that 'only exists on DVD.' Do you want to watch it tonight? Maybe a movie?"

"Well," I said, slowly. "We can watch a movie at your apartment. I will not be able to help with your other request."

"May I ask why you just gave me a vague and cryptic answer?"

"I'm locked out of my apartment."

Silence for just a moment, then, "What?"

"Technically, I'm not locked out, the door just won't open. But don't worry, it'll only be like that for two weeks."

"Two weeks? What-"

"Before you worry, I'll be okay, I actually have a small bag packed in my car in case this ever happened." That is the truth, actually. I joke that I have a 'go bag' in case the FBI ever gets too close to catching me. Luckily, I don't have to worry about that because I've never done anything illegal.

Other than jaywalking sometimes. In my defense, I only do it when there's no one on the road. So...ha.

"That's mildly concerning, but okay."

"Yeah, I'll be fine in my car. I should actually go set that up, talk to you later."

I hung up.

I think that went well. I found a subtle way to include that I will be living in my car without worrying him because my tone was even. That's effective communication. Now, I have the last word because-

Michael called me back.

Oh.

I forgot he could do that.

"I'm sorry I don't think I heard you right," Michael stated as soon as I picked up. "Did you just say you'd be sleeping in your car for the next two weeks?"

"Uh..."

"Ev, your car is nice, but it's practically the size of a Kia. How will you be comfortable sleeping in it?"

"I won't be. But, before you say anything, I have a plan. When I sleep bad, I'll just have coffee at work. See? Problem solved."

Although he wasn't standing in front of me, I could practically feel him deadpanning on the other end of the line.

"You can stay with me, if you want."

"Michael-"

"Here me out," Michael began. "I have a two bedroom apartment, so you can have the guest room. And, the biggest factor in all of this, you won't have to sleep inside your car. It's so unsafe. What would happen if someone tried to break into your car while you were sleeping?"

"I'd run them over."

"Although that's a solid option, I'd avoid any illegal actions."

I opened my mouth to protest again, but Michael beat me to speech, "Before you say whatever you're about to say, it's no problem. Seriously. I'd enjoy having company too."

I smiled. He really is a teddy bear. The people at Trader Joe's last week don't know that after the incident with the shopping carts, but I know.

"Okay," I said at last. "Fine, I'll stay with you. But you have to promise to kick me out the second I become too much of a hassle. Deal?"

"I don't think we'll reach that point, but deal."

"Perfect," I responded. I was about to say something when I saw Adam then the corner. "Hold on," I told Michael.

"Hey asshole, give me my earrings."

"I don't have-"

"Yes, you do. I can see them in your pocket."

"Fine," Adam walked over to me and handed me my one nice pair of earrings. I think all of my earrings are nice, but these are the only ones made out of real gold, so I don't think nice is used sparingly.

"I didn't steal anything else, all of your shit is cheap."

"You really are a joy to be around. Now where's my fish? I don't see you holding him."

"Oh yeah." Adam opened his backpack and pulled out a water bottle. What the hell-

"You out my fish in a water bottle?" I practically yelled.

"I couldn't find the carrier."

"It's right next to his tank," I said, exasperated.

"Oh, oops."

"Just," I paused, regaining any semblance of my composure, "give him to me."

Adam held out his hand he just used to hand me poor Wasabi, "Now, where's my money."

"Oh, I'm not paying you. First you tried to rob me of the one nice thing I own and then you put my fish in a water bottle purely out of spite. Now go, before I call the cops of you."

Adam glared at me before walking away.

"Sorry, Wasabi," I told him. This poor fish.

"Um, Ev?"

Oh shit. Michael's still on the phone with me.

"Hi. Sorry, my delinquent neighbor tried to rob me after I told him to break into my apartment to save Wasabi."

"I don't know what to say."

"That's okay. But, truly, thank you. For letting me stay with you, I mean. I appreciate it."

"Of course. See you tonight?"

"See you tonight."

~~~

HEYYYYYYYYYYYYYYYYYYYThis chapter is significantly longer than intended. I started writing it then I vibed with it more than I thought I would.I'm glad Wasabi made it out alive.Now Michael and Evelyn are going to be living together for two weeks, which,
~~~

looking at the timeline, overlaps on Ev's birthday. I do wonder what Michael will do.And they have a movie date next chapter and they'll do domestic stuff.Derek's been real quiet recently, I wonder if he'll stay that way...Lastly, a very sincere thank you for 6k reads, I truly appreciate it.

Chapter 19 - A Perplexed Parisian's Predicament

Chapter Song: Until I Found You by Stephen Sanchez

EvelynI'm a terrible person.

I can't believe I just bribed a literal child to break into my apartment. What kind of behavior does that teach? Answer: the bad kind.

Oh shit.

I don't think he locked my window. So help me, if I come back and he stole something I swear I will...

I don't know, actually. But I'll do something.

I won't call the cops on him or anything, but maybe I'll throw a water balloon or something at him. I'll take suggestions.

~~~

"Ev, hey," Michael greeted.

"Hey."

"Is that all you have?" Michael asked, eyeing the bag slung over my shoulder. It consisted of one pair of shorts, one pair of jeans, two bras,
~~~

and five pairs of underwear.When I was packing my little 'go bag,' I probably should've packed more.

Oh well.

"Yeah," I shrugged, "I couldn't exactly go into my apartment to get more."

"Shit, sorry. I didn't mean-"

"It's okay, I'm just joking." Michael still looked tense though, almost as if he was nervous.

"Are you okay?"

"What? Yeah, I'm fine. Come in."

Michael stepped to the side so I could walk in and I was amazed. Last time I was here I was delirious with a fever and only conscious maybe twenty percent of the time, so I felt like this is the first time that I'm actually seeing his apartment.

It's small, but it's nice. There's an open floor plan, or at least as open as it can be in a two bedroom apartment, and everything in his house matches. Each shade of grey or dark blue works really well each other, the light and dark tones of the room complete balanced so it doesn't feel like I'm standing in cave.

Not to be sexist or anything, but most guys don't know about complementary colors.

Michael is not most guys. In more than one sense of the phrase.

It's kind of funny though, there's next to no color in his apartment other the-

Oh my God.

A fish tank.

"I figured Wasabj might need a place to say," Michael said, noting where I was staring. "Is this okay?"

Does he even need to ask? He bought a fish tank for Wasabi. It's not the fact that he bought it that's leaving me speechless, it's his thoughtfulness.

And now Wasabi doesn't need to live the next to weeks in a water bottle or tall bowl. He has his own fish tank.

"Michael, thank you."

"Yeah, it's no problem," he shrugged. I couldn't help but see the tension in his shoulders lessen and his stance become more relaxed.

Was he nervous about what I would think of his apartment? Of this incredible gesture that he's shown?

"Michael," I took his hands in my own. "Thank you."

Michael stared down at our joined hands, then back up at me. Technically, he was still looking down. But I didn't dwell on the technicalities. I pushed myself up a little bit and gave him a soft, gentle kiss.

I felt him smile against my lips and whisper, "That was nice."

"Oh yeah?" I mumbled, kissing him again.

"Yeah."

I pulled away and leaned my forehead against his, enjoying this moment between us. Everything just felt so easy. I don't have to pretend or change the myself just so he'd like me. I can simply be.

Michael lifted my chin up so he could look at me, "Sometimes I can't believe that you're real. It's the quiet moments when I think that l maybe I made you up, because this, is perfect."

I smiled at him, "If any one of us is hallucinating this relationship, it's me."

Michael leaned down and kissed me again, "That felt pretty real to me."

"Me too."

~~~

Michael's clothes are so fucking comfy. I feel like I'm being wrapped in a million hugs.

And it smells like him too.

Since I didn't have any sleepwear on me, Michael let me have some of his shirts, a sweatshirt, and a pair of his dark green flannel pants.

I opted for the grey t shirt and the green flannel.

Maybe it's just wearing my boyfriend's clothes or wearing clothes that are big on me, but I'm so insanely comfy I can't take it.

I walk out of the guest bedroom and see Michael at the kitchen counter. He's wearing dark blue flannel pants a black t shirt.

Of course he's wearing dark colors.

"Hey," I spoke after a moment, seeing as he hasn't noticed me yet.

"Oh, hey. Do you like the-" Michael stopped. His eyes widened and he stared at me, his mouth slightly agape.

"Is everything okay?" I found myself asking for the second time that evening.

"Yeah," Michael said, breathlessly. "I'm good."

"Good," I smiled. "What are you making?"

Michael cleared his throat, "Soup. Tomato bisque, actually. It's my mom's recipe. All I have to do is get the-shit."
~~~

"I take it that's not good."

"I forgot the baguette," Michael pouted.

I couldn't help but laugh, "Michael, I say this with all of the affection in my heart, but that's practically sacrilege. You're French, and you forgot the baguette."

"Shut up."

"I'm sorry, I'm not trying to be intensive or to stereotype you, but you have to admit it, the whole thing is kind of funny."

"Yeah, yeah," Michael said grabbing his keys. "Bye. I'm going to go get the bread."

"Bye! Be back soon, mon chéri."

"Uh huh," Michael closed the door and I locked the door. It really is a miracle to handle a door that isn't a literal safety hazard.

I walked up to Wasabi's tank and stared at him, "How did we get so lucky, little guy?"

I was so busy daydreaming that when I heard a knock on the door it scared the shit out of me. Michael is already back? Wow, how long was I staring at Wasabi?

I opened the door and was greeted by...

"Evelyn," Derek's eyes lit up with sparkling amusement, taking note of not only my presence in Michael's apartment, but clothes I was wearing. Michael's clothes. "What are you doing here?"

"My apartment door is busted, so I'm staying with Michael for the time being."

"How thoughtful of him. And what a shame about the door. Funny how stuff like that just...happens."

"Yeah," I said slowly, kind of confused. "My door is just shitty I guess."

Derek shrugged and reached into his backpack. "Here," he handed me a bag that said 'Happy Birthday' in sparkly font. "For you."

"Thank you, that's really thoughtful of you," I said, taking the bag from his hand.

"No problem, I was just visiting Michael and I was going to give him this to give to you."

"That's great! Did you ever get to see him the other day?"

"I did. We had a fun little chat. I even put a really good tablet in his water, it made it sparkling and some cool shit."

"That does sound cool."

"You know what? Here," he took a tablet out of his backpack and stuck it into my bag. "I know this is weird, but I just come across strong. Here's a show of good faith." Derek took out another packet and stuffed it in his mouth. He snapped his jaw a few times then smiled.

"Uh, thanks."

Derek winked at me before his gaze shifted to someone to my right. I took a step out the door to see who Derek was looking at, only to see Michael. He stood frozen in the doorway, unmoving with a grocery bag in his hand.

"Michael," Derek said, sliding his arm around my shoulders. "It's so great to see you."

~~~
~~~

HEYYYYYYYYYYYYYWriting the fluff earlier made me want to die because I probably never will experience anything like that. I hope I do and I hope you all do to, if that's what you want.And up next is the long awaited confrontation and the truth comes out about Derek. Oh, and it's all in Michael's POV.I want to give a shout-out to your comments were so funny, seriously. Thank you. Well, that was fun. I'm dead tired but I'll probably be scrolling on TikTok for another two hours, so I should be around.Until next time, bye!

Chapter 20 - Contradictory Bread

Chapter Song: Grace by Lewis Capaldi

MichaelWhat the fuck.

I couldn't move. I couldn't do anything but stand there like an idiot holding a fucking baguette.

Evelyn smiled at me awkwardly and shimmied her way out of Derek's grasp. Although she had moved, Derek let his hand linger on her shoulder for a few moments longer than necessary, staring at me with a conniving, devil's smile.

"What are you doing here?" It was less of a question and more or a demand.

"I was just here to bring Evelyn a birthday gift. And to say hi to you, of course."

Uh huh.

I was surprised I didn't see the sparkly bag in her hand, it stood out like a sore thumb.

"Derek," I started, "kindly get the fuck out of here."

"But I just got here, it'd be rude to kick me out so soon."

Ev walked over to me, intertwining my hand with hers. She must've noticed something was wrong because she whispered, "Is everything okay?"

"Honestly, no. But I'll tell you about it when he leaves."

Evelyn smiled at me and, fuck, if it didn't make want to smile too.

Forgetting Derek and all of his bullshit, I gave her hand a little squeeze and smiled. I honestly couldn't help it.

"Interesting," Derek murmured.

"Thanks for the gift, Derek. We actually have plans to go see a movie in," Evelyn checked her phone, "Half an hour. So we should get going."

Derek nodded, "I understand. I wouldn't want to take up any more of your time. It was nice seeing you again, Ev."

He did not just call her Ev-

Wait.

Again? He's talked to her before?

My jaw tightened as he walked past me and put a hand on my shoulder, "It was great seeing you again too, Michael."

Once he turned the corner, Ev looked at me, "I feel like I might've missed a few chapters."

I chuckled, "Yeah, maybe just a few."

"Care to share with the rest of the class? If not, that's okay. I'll wait until you're ready."

"I don't deserve you," I whispered as I kissed her, taking a moment to bask in her splendor.

"Come on, let's go inside, yeah?"

"Yeah."

~~~

I've been sitting on my couch watching tv with Evelyn for ten minutes already and I'm at a lost for words.

What do I even say?

I can't just begin with, 'so, that guy you saw was my brother. By the way, we hate each other and I'm pretty sure he's a drug dealer or some shady shit.'

I'm kind of on a time crunch too because the fucking bread needs to bake in the overnight for eighteen minutes before we can eat it. Which, by the way, is moronic. It's also false advertising.

Why not just make the bread already baked so people can eat it right away and avoid awkward conversations about their shady worm of a brother?

I sighed, catching Ev's attention. She put her hand on my thigh in silent acknowledgment of...me. How does she do that? It's like she just knows. Maybe she has superpowers or something, because her being able to tell my mood based on a sigh alone is uncanny.

"Ev?"

"Hm?" Ev hummed in response, her head resting on my shoulder.

"I want to tell you about my brother but..."

But what?

But I don't want you to think any less of me?
~~~

But I don't want you to leave me when you hear what he made me do?

But I'm scared that you'll leave me once you realize I'm a bad person?

I'm scared that you'll look at me the way you do in my nightmares, where your eyes full of anger and disgust.

"It's okay," Evelyn whispered. "You don't have to tell me anything if you don't want to. I can wait until you're ready."

"Fuck. Okay, I'll just start. When I was younger, my dad left Derek, my mom and I. Derek moved out of our house about a year after my dad went back to France. It was just my mom and I for six years before I moved out. Derek was always on the rebellious side, but nothing more concerning than normal teenage drama. I should've known something was going on the first time he asked me for money.

"Derek knocked on the door to my mom's house and asked me if he could have five hundred dollars to fix his car because he couldn't afford it," I shook my head. "He was such a liar, I should've seen it. Barely two months later he came to me again, asking for more money; Almost one thousand dollars this time.

"His excuse was his pipes burst in his apartment and he needed to fix it. The next time he asked me for money and gave some bullshit excuse, I said no. He was pissed. I've seen him aggressive, but that was hyper aggressive, it honestly scared me. There was something in his eyes that day, I don't know if it was new or if I'd just never seen it. But," I swallowed. "It was dark, Ev. He threatened me. He said that if I didn't give him the money he'd hurt me and my mom. I could care less about what happens to me, but my mom? Our mom. Who does that?"

I felt Ev staring at me, but I couldn't meet her eyes. I couldn't bring myself to see that look of disappointment that I know is in her eyes. I can't.

"I gave him the money, then and every time after that. I couldn't exactly call the cops on him, it's my word against his. I tried to reason with him every time I saw him, but he wouldn't budge. I don't even know what he was doing with the money, but I didn't care as long as he stayed away from me.

"One day, though, I saw on the news that a group of five guys were suspected for armed robbery. Derek's face was on the screen. When he came to my house I turned him in. He went through so much hell in jail. He was in the infirmary what felt like every other day. He hated me for what I did. So did my dad, too. As soon as he found out what I did he was pissed. He probably yelled at me for an hour before he hung up. I couldn't bring myself to hang up on him first, I just sat there and let him bulldoze over me.

"And, I know what I did was the right thing to do, but I hated myself for it. How could I turn in my own brother? What kind of person does that make me? Maybe I'm just like him: Manipulative and selfish and-"

"Michael," Evelyn said, her voice soft, "Look at me."

I closed my eyes and shook my head, feeling the tears starting. I've never said any of that to anyone, much less actively thought about it.

It hurt. He made me feel like the only thing I was good for was what I could do for him.

I felt so small. Then and now.

"Michael," Ev repeated. "Please?"

It was then that I looked at her.

I didn't see what I expected.

Her eyes were understanding, her expression warm and comforting. She brought her hand up to my cheeks, wiping the tears that had begun to fall. She smiled softly and said, "It's not your fault. You are not the one to blame for all of this. You helped your mom and you did everything in your power to help your bother. It's not your fault he didn't listen. You did everything right."

I couldn't hold it in any more. Her words and her eyes-

God, her eyes. There was so much kindness and trust in them that I couldn't take it anymore. It was all too much.

I cried.

She pulled me into her arms and I just cried.

"You're wrong," I hiccuped between sobs. Feeling her hands move so delicately through my hair, giving me comfort I didn't deserve. "It's all my fault. I should've-"

"You did everything right. Nothing is your fault."

"It is," I said shaking my head, "They were right and I shouldn't have been such a shitty brother."

"Michael, listen to me. Please. None of what happened is your fault. Derek manipulated and threatened you, there was nothing more you could've done. And whatever anyone said to make you feel like you're a selfish and shitty brother can fight m themselves because you are the exact opposite of that. Michael, you're a good person."

I couldn't help but laugh. It sounded more like I was choking than laughing, but I made my point.

"How do you do that?" I ask, finally looking up at her.

"Do what?"

"Be so kind."

Ev smiled, "You make it easy."

I smiled, wiping the tears from my eyes, and sniffling. Pulling back, I can see that pretty much the top of her shirt is soaked. "Shit, sorry, I got your shirt wet."

"Technically, it's your shirt."

"It looks better on you. Do you want to keep it?"

"I won't tell you. Call it my way of keeping you on your toes."

And, suddenly, I was whole again.

~~~

HEYYYYYYYYYYYFirst, I'm sorry for falling off of the face of the earth and taking forever to update.I've had so many exams to study for I think my mind is literally going to explode.I'm running on two hours of sleep and a cup of coffee, so I'm pretty much dead.Okay, this chapter was a little bit sad. Michael needs a hug. The next one will be happier, I promise. Next chapter will be soon!
~~~

Chapter 21 - Birthday Surprises

Chapter Song: Keep Driving by Harry Styles

EvelynShit.

I'm twenty one.

What the hell?

I'm twenty one.

Okay, I need to avoid an existential crisis before I mourn the loss of my childhood. Is that dramatic? Maybe to some people. But these are my feelings and I refuse to let them be discredited.

So, ha.

Okay, now I really need to avoid that existential crisis. People always say 'go to your happy place.' What's my happy place?

Christmas, bread, Michael-

Michael. His laugh, his smile, his eyes. God, his eyes. Even his comfy clothes that smell like him. Everything. It's all him. And now, in his apartment, it's us.

It's strange how that works sometimes. A relationship, I mean. How can someone can just slip into another person's life so easily? I don't even know when it happened. We just seemed to fall into step besides one another. I don't know if it's us living together for the past week or how well we get along, but every time I'm around him I get this feeling I can't quite describe.

I think it's love.

But I've never been in love before, so I don't know what it feels like since I have nothing to compare it to. But what I feel when I'm with Michael, it's exactly like what I imagine love feels like.

It's a heart swelling, all consuming feeling that makes me want to laugh and cry at the same time. It's hoping not to get caught after staring for a few moments too long. It's holding his hand for a moment longer than necessary because I don't want to let go. It's being intrigued by the smallest and most insignificant of actions. It's the indescribable thrill and fear of walking across a tightrope, but the security of knowing that no matter what, the tightrope won't waver. And neither will I.

Maybe it is love.

Or...waffles?

Why does it smell like waffles?

I creaked open my (temporary) bedroom door and popped my head outside. There were gold streamers hanging in various places around the apartment and gold confetti on the floor, making the whole room shimmer. I smiled at the vase of fresh irises in a gold vase on the kitchen table.

I think I see a theme here.

Michael was standing in the kitchen, staring at a waffle maker with so much concentration that I wouldn't be surprised if his stare made it explode. He looked cute, actually. Well, he always looks cute, but there was something different about him today. He was wearing black jeans and an emerald green button up long sleeve, probably thrown over a white t shirt. His curls were still unruly, but they seemed to be in place (for once).

Slowly, I walked up to him. I didn't want to break his concentration on...whatever he was concentrating on, but I also wanted to see how long was left on the waffles because I'm starving.

I tapped Michael on the shoulder and he jumped backwards, hitting his wrist on the counter.I chuckled slightly and wrapped my arms around his waist once his shock filled eyes met my amused ones.

"You're jumpy this morning."

"And you," Michael said, covering my eyes with his hand, "are not supposed to be awake yet. You always sleep in until around 9. It's only 8:30."

"We'll, yeah," I said, moving blindly as Michael pushed me out of the kitchen. "But I couldn't sleep. I smelled waffles."

I heard a door close behind me and micheal took his hands off of my eyes. "How much did you see outside?"

"Would you believe me if I said nothing?"

"No."

"In that case, I saw everything."

"Shit. I wanted it to be a surprise."

"It is!" I exclaimed, grabbing his hand, "and I'm sure I didn't see everything, I wasn't looking for that long. In all honesty, I was looking at you."

Michael blushed and it was the cutest thing I've ever seen. "I, un, I need to go check on the waff-I mean, food. I'll come get you in a minute, okay?"

"As long as it's only a minute."

Michael smiled and shook his head, "Only a minute, I promise."

~~~

Michael did not take only a minute.

He took ten minutes. (But I don't hold that against him.) From what I could tell, he burnt the waffles and had to start over. Then he (maybe) broke something. I'm not one hundred percent sure about that one, but I thought I heard a crashing sound followed by Michael swearing.

When Michael walked into my room he told me to close my eyes as he led me through his apartment. He positioned me so I faced what I could only guess was a window. Or the air vent. Either option seems viable since air was hitting my face.

"Open your eyes."

I was expecting something, I don't know what, but something, and there was nothing. Just the same view I saw every-

Oh. Oh.

I'm an idiot. There was a paper taped to the window frame saying 'turn around.'
~~~

I obliged and couldn't help the gasp I let out. Light trickled in from the windows and reflected against the confetti on the floor, bathing not just Michael and I, but the whole room, in an array of gold light.

It was incredible.

"Michael, you didn't have to. It's beautiful."

"And so are you."

"Stop it," I laughed, blushing like a madwoman.

"Never," Michael smiled back. "You mean the world to me and I wanted to do something for you."

I shook my head smiling.

"Come on," Michael started, pulling me towards the kitchen. "I have the whole day planned out. Starting with breakfast."

I will pretend that I'm surprised and not like I've been salivating over these waffles for the past 15 minutes because they smell really good.

With a flourishing land movement, Michael gestured to the kitchen and the waffles on the counter. There was an absurd amount of whipped cream on top of them and I dipped my finger in it and ate some. "My favorite kind of sugary fuel."

Michael leaned in and kissed me, licking his lips after. "I think it might be mine too," he said, kissing me again.

Oh my God.

Oh my God. Oh my God. Oh. My. God.

Michael pulled away and looked at me-well, not me, my lips. I could feel my cheeks burning up, my face undoubtably turning a new vibrant shade of red.

"Stop it," I playfully pushed him aside. You're distracting me from eating my waffles."

"Fine. I'll let you enjoy my culinary masterpiece. But we are kind of on the clock, so would it be possible if you were ready to go by 11:30?"

"What's at 11:30?"

~~~

(THIS NEXT PART IS SPOILER FREE - I WROTE THIS BEFORE PART 2 CAME OUT)

(Sorry for the aggressive all caps, I need the text to stand out because I don't want anyone to think I'm spoiling anything.)

"How about we watch Stranger Things at midnight?"

"It's a good thing it doesn't come out on my birthday," I said, staring at the window, trying to figure out where we're going.

"Why?"

"Because if Steve Harrington dies then I will throw myself off of a cliff."

Michael smiled, still staring at the road. "But whatever would I do without you?"

"You'd take care of Wasabi. So help me if I see him in the afterlife right after I die then I will come back and haunt you forever."

"Dually noted. But do know that every time I see Wasabi he'll remind me of you and I'll be depressed."

"Good. As you should be. Now shut up I want to listen to this song in peace and quiet."

"I'm wounded that-"
~~~

"Shhhh."

There are two ways I sing when I hear a song I like while I'm in a car. The first way is I become a complete menace and scream the lyrics, undoubtedly harassing the other person in the car with me. The second way is a slightly more calm approach, somewhat conservatively, depending on how well I know the person.

Either way, they are both with the same energy as a Broadway performance.

For instance, if Tolerate It by Taylor Swift plays, expect me to be singing through tears. But if Last Christmas by Wham! plays, prepare to be sick of me because I will pour my heart and soul into that song.

It all depends on the song. Do I laugh? Do I cry? Do I scream? Do I accidentally drive myself and an unlucky passenger off of a cliff because I'm so invested in the music? Well, hopefully not that last one, that wouldn't be good. But if I die listening to my favorite song, I'm okay with that.

But there are instances where a song feels...right. When the lyrics hit you so hard in just the right moment that you're knocked off your feet.

Keep Driving by Harry Styles feels like that. The right song in the right moment.

Maple syrup,Coffee, pancakes for twoHash brown, egg yolkI will always love you

"A small concern with how the engine soundsWe held darkness in withheld cloudsI would ask, "Should we just keep driving?"" I sang with a smile.

"Should we just keep driving?" I heard Michael sing softly.

"No way! You've listened to the album?"

"Yes, you made me listen to it all."

"I know that," I replied sarcastically. "But there's no way you memorized the words after two listens. I knew it! You're a Harry Styles fan."

Michael opened his mouth to speak, but I stopped him. "Ah, don't try and deny it. I know you'd be lying."

"How so?"

"Because my bullshit detector is always keyed up to a million. That's how I survive."

"Good to know."

"Where are we going anyway?" I ask, looking out the window. We've been driving around the city for a long time. While the drive has been fun, I also really want to know where we're going.

"It's a surprise."

"I don't like you anymore."

Michael chuckled, "We're almost there."

Michael took a sudden sharp right and we ended up in a hidden courtyard. There was a staircase leading underground and an ominous emptiness to the courtyard. I narrowed my eyes at Michael, "Did you bring me here to murder me?"

"No. And I'm starting to take offense to you thinking I'm a murderer."

"In this world, you can never be too careful. That's why I know self defense. And offense."

"Self offense?" Michael asked, raising an eyebrow.

"Yeah. In the event someone's harassing me or being a jackass, I'll just punch that person in the face. Or kick him in the balls."

"Have I ever told you that you scare me?"

"Not enough."

Michael got out of the car and I followed, waking frighteningly closer to the creepy stairs. I really wanted to say something smart, but I was focusing on not losing my nerve and either running away or falling down the stairs.

When we reached the bottom of the stairs, there was a black door with linear gold accents on it. It felt very 1920's.

Michael opened it to reveal the most beautiful movie theatre I've ever seen.

"It was build in the early 1920's as a speakeasy type place. Eventually it got turned into a movie theatre, but the owners made sure to keep the 20's influence in the building."

I ran my hand across the gold pillars and designs on the walls. It was so beautiful. Gatsby would leave his mansion for this place, it was that beautiful.

"What do you think?"

"I love it. Thank you."

Michael smiled and looked at his shoes.

"What movie are we seeing?" I asked.

"Sabrina."

"Shut up. You did not. You did not get us tickets in the coolest movie theatre on the planet to see one of my favorite movies ever."

"I did."

"Oh my God! Have I already said thank you?"

"Yes. Now come on, we don't want to miss our showing."

~~~
~~~

Chapter 22 - The Great British Baking Shit Show

Chapter Song: The Pool by Stephen Sanchez

MichaelGod, I love her.

I love her so much I can't even articulate it. Love is far too small of a word to convey all that I feel for her. I know it's cheesy and an unoriginal, cliche like thing to say, but it's true. When I imagine myself happy, she's there. She's always there. In my thoughts, my dreams, my future, it's all her.

It's all Evelyn.

What else can I say about her other than she's the feeling of listening to my favorite song?

It's so stupid. It's so fucking stupid that this is happening to me. I was just fine with my black coffee and 'lifeless apartment.' But no, she had to come and ruin it all. She had to smile and laugh and be the most incredible person I've ever met.

If I'm being completely honest, I wasn't fully watching the movie tonight; all I could see was her. She looked as beautiful as she always does, but she was radiant tonight. The light in her eyes is bright enough to illuminate my entire life, leaving me in a haze of bliss day in and day out.

If I could give her just a fraction of the joy she makes me feel every day, then I'll be one step closer to deserving her. She deserves the world every day, but I want to see if I can make the world seem a little bit more beautiful today.

When we first arrived, I could see it on her face how much she loved the movie theatre, and that wasn't even the best part of what I have planned.

~~~

"I hate surprises."

"No, you don't."

"Again with the gaslighting."

"I'm not," I said defensively, (minority) panicking. "I know you told me once that you love surprises because-"

"Michael," Evelyn interrupted. "I know. I'm just kidding."

"Yeah, yeah," I grunted as she laughed.

I had a blindfold over her eyes and led her into a small bakery. It took time, begging, and three of my paychecks to afford but I was able to pull it off.

Honestly, if Ev doesn't like this I don't know what I'll do. Maybe I'll die.

"Okay, open your eyes."
~~~

Evelyn removed the blindfold and her jaw dropped. The whole room had been decorated like the tent from the Great British Baking Show. There were little British flags, cute aprons, and bowls full of everything needed to give you diabetes.

Are the calories worth it? Absolutely.

Is the look on her face making it extra worth it? Fucking yes.

"You did this?"

I nodded.

Her eyes watered, "For me?"

"No, for your evil twin."

She laughed through tears, "Oh shut up. What are we baking?"

"Tiramisu."

"Shut the fuck up. You did not find a recipe for tiramisu."

"I did."

"Oh my God!" She yelled, hugging me. "Thank you. Thank you. Thank you."

"It was no problem, really."

Lie.

"You liar," she smiled. Shit, she's good. Maybe she's getting too good at reading me. Or she's psychic. I say that last option is very valid.

Just like somehow she knew I'd like that sugary monstrosity she gives me every morning. And last week she somehow knew that I wanted to watch Nightmare Before Christmas in the middle of July. She's psychic, I know it.

"Come on," Ev said, pulling me towards the aprons. "You get the sparkly one."

"I got that one for you. The shiny one's for me."

"Not anymore. And you'll look radiant in sparkles."

I grunted and she laughed.

God, that laugh.

"Step one," Ev read, "using an electric mixer mix egg yolks and sugar. That shouldn't be too hard."

It wasn't that hard, actually.

Step two on the other hand...

"How the fuck do you make 'medium peaks?' What even are those?" I asked, reading step two.

"Have you really not paid attention every time we've watched baking shows? You mix the stuff until it's firm. It's the one where you test if it's ready by flipping it upside down and seeing if it keeps it's shape."

"What happens if it doesn't?"

"You cry. Or die. Maybe a bit of both."

"Sounds healthy."

"Oh, definitely. Now, squat down."

I furrow my brows, "why?"

Ev smiled wickedly. "We need to test the mascarpone for stiff peaks."

She's lucky I love her.

I got on my knees and looked up at her, waiting. No, not just waiting, praying. Praying for the opportunity to never leave her side and to spend every walking moment surrounded by her beauty. Because that's what she is: beautiful. Her beauty isn't just physical, it's spiritual. She has the kindest soul I've ever known and spark far brighter than any fire.

"Michael? Hello?" Ev said, her voice sounding distant. Her voice. It's like I'm a kid fawning over their middle school crush. We've been dating for almost two months and I still feel just as excited to be around her as I did when I first met her. It's almost-

My thoughts are cut off by her lips on mine. She tastes like sugar and suddenly I'm hungry for more, more, more.

But as quickly as she's there, she's gone. Whatever look was on my face must've been priceless because she stared at me and laughed. "You zoned out and I couldn't get your attention. I knew a way that could snap you back to reality."

"It worked."

"Really? I had no idea. And look up."

I looked up and saw that she was holding the bowl over my head and nothing spilled out. I chuckled, firm peaks.

"You're really good baking."

"Not really. I just have a fear of failure."

I don't know what to say to that. I mean, me too, but how do I even- just how?

"Just kidding. Partly. Now get up, we still have steps 3-8 to work on."

"On a scale of one to ten how difficult is the rest?"

"Maybe a 7. And your grading scale is boring. It should be 'on a scale of I'm okay to I want to die how would you rate this?'"

"That seems a bit...extreme."

"Is it extreme or practical?"

"Practical," I said after a moment. "But what would a seven be?"

"It's 'I'm beginning to entertain the idea of giving up and laying in bed forever.'"

I stayed quiet for a moment. How does she always come up with this stuff? I'm impressed and slightly concerned.

Something hit me on my arm. Ev threw a whisk at me.

"If you don't come help then you don't get to eat any of this once it's done."

"Okay, okay, I'm coming."

~~~

We decided to take the tiramisu to my apartment once we finished making it. If we were contestants on a baking show we would've been eliminated because it took us forever to finish it. And because we burned the first one and had to start over.

Who knew that making a tiramisu was so difficult?

Everyone but us apparently.

As soon as we got to my apartment, Ev ran to her room to change into her pjs. She said something about only being able to look cute for a few hours before she "turned back into a troll."

I insisted that she never looks like a troll but she disagreed and said that I was just being polite (which I wasn't, I think she looks beautiful all the time) and stated that she didn't believe me.
~~~

I'll change her mind one day.

"So," Ev started as she walked into the room, plopping down on the couch right next to me and grabbing her slice of tiramisu. "What should we watch?"

"It's your birthday, so by law it's your choice."

"Oooo, that's a lot of power. I can pick anything?"

"Anything."

"How about Little Women?"

"Whatever you want."

Ev smiled and kissed me, "It's not every day that boyfriends willingly watch Little Women with their girlfriend. But, seriously, thank you. Today was perfect."

"You're perfect," I hummed.

"Shut up or I'll stab you with my fork."

"That wouldn't stop me from complimenting you. Nothing could."

"Oh yeah?" Ev questioned. "What about this?"

And she kissed me.

Again.

And again.

And again.

"Nope," I whispered, pulling away slightly. "You're-"

She kissed me again and I smiled against her lips.

"Why do I feel like this was all an elaborate ploy to get me to kiss you?"

"I don't know. I'm just trying not to be stabbed my the madwoman with the fork."

"Very funny," Ev said sarcastically. "Now, watch the movie or I might actually stab you."

"Yes ma'am."

Chapter 23 - Edible Arraignments

Chapter Song: The Man by Taylor Swift

EvelynI sound like a broken record.

My inner monologue and every brain cell in my brain is a combination of the usual thoughts: Harry Styles songs, the urge to say random words with a British accent, the ending of La La Land, and food of any and all varieties.

Yet, a new category has decided to make an appearance: love.

I always joked that love is meaningless, but I think I was on to something. Love is meaningless in the sense that a four letter word doesn't convey enough meaning to describe how one feels when they're in love. Yet, the word has enough meaning that it's frightening.

How can I love and be so afraid at the same time?

This is too existential crisis-y for me, so I'm going to avoid my problems instead of facing them.

...yeah.

~~~

"Priya, answer me honestly. If I put in my notice right now, would you leave with me?"

"Hell yeah, Leah is a demon. Maybe even Satan Herself," Priya griped.

Even though Priya has only been working at Clairo's for four months, I've come to the conclusion that I'd die without her. After our shifts we have what we call 'Shit on Sanity' where we take five minutes after each shift to just vent about everything that made us want to die that day. It's great.

"If you would quit, what would you do next?" I ask.

"Either museum curator at the Louvre or boxing coach. What about you?"

"Zookeeper to penguins or I'd train myself to do something cool where I'd be respected. I don't get enough of that here."

"I feel that. What I would kill to be able to finish a sentence without being interrupted by a man who thinks he knows more than me."

"I'd toast to that if I had a drink."

"I'd get drunk at the end of every shift if we worked at bar. Anyway, what are you going to do once classes start again?" Priya asked.

"Die."

She laughed, "yeah, that sounds about right. At least your school doesn't have a roach problem."

At the end of last semester, the city was doing construction near Priya's school and there was a bunch of roaches that crawled out
~~~

of the sewers onto her campus. People were finding roaches in the dorms and they even crawled into a few peoples backpacks.

It sounds like nightmare material to me.

"Yeah," I said. "No roaches where I'm going. Just depression and anxiety."

"Sounds like college."

~~~

My apartment is fixed.

I loved living with Michael, but oh my god I missed my apartment. Yes, it had its quirks, but I love it. I grabbed my 'go bag' and Wasabi while Michael was at work and texted him saying that I could move back in and I desperately needed to wear my own clothes again.

And I want to see if that little shit teenager either A: came back through the window and stole something. Or B, left the window open and left my apartment to be the new home for a family of crows, possums, rats, or another miscellaneous creature.

I wouldn't doubt it if there were roaches in there since karma is not my boyfriend.

I grab the key and half expect my door to explode or fall on me, but nothing happens. The door just clicks unlocked. I don't think that's ever happened on the first try before. In all honesty I'm scared to open the door.

But everything's fine.

Wasabi's fish tank is where it should be, my TV and laptop are still there, and oh thank God. No one stole my microwave.
~~~

I will be the first to admit that I am not a chef. Although, I like to pretend that I am by adding Italian herbs to my microwave meals to make myself feel better.

Wait wait wait.

No. Fucking. Way.

That piece of shit stood my coffee maker.

Yes, it sounds trivial because I work at a coffee shop. But there is no way in hell I'm paying for coffee every day at an overpriced coffee joint where I only get a fifty cent employee discount. I'm broke enough as it is, I can't spend my money on coffee everyday.

I would like to believe that Lorelai Gilmore and I have a few fundamental things in common. The most predominant of the two being that we would die without coffee and cease to function on any level. Water is overrated. I will not sit down at eight in the morning and drink a hot cup of water and think, "wow, everything suddenly makes sense. I know all of life's secrets." What I will do it sit down at eight in the morning and think both "I'm so glad I have coffee at this ungodly hour" and "wow, I love coffee."

Considering my bank account is about one spontaneous decision away from me having to quit school and work full time, I think one of the coffee machines at work might "accidentally" break and I throw it in the dumpster but put it in the trunk of my car once my shift ends.

~~~

"Leah, the coffee machine broke."

"Yeah," Priya added. "I couldn't get it so start either."

"Just throw it out, I don't really care."
~~~

"Okay, I'll throw it in the dumpster," I reply.

Leah sighs and stares at the machine, shaking her head. "I knew I shouldn't have moved to California."

Priya and I stare at each other, trying not to laugh at the casual...tr auma dumping? Randomness of her comment? All the above, most likely.

The only thing that I truly knew for certain was that I just got a new coffee machine.

~~~
~~~

Chapter 24 - Dad Jokes and Daddy Issues

Chapter Song: Brutal by Olivia Rodrigo

EvelynI love Christmas.

The whole holiday season is the best time of year. The food, the lights, the decorations, the music - it's all absolutely perfect. Objectively, it's the best holiday. In any movie, book, tv show, they never skip Christmas. It's a fun addition to any and everything.

Unlike Thanksgiving. For thanksgiving, people just watch Charlie Brown or Friends. And there's no music. If I were to ask anyone on the street to name a Thanksgiving song, most people won't be able to.

Bye with Christmas, there's an array or songs to choose from. They're good to listen to all year long too. I could put on Last Christmas by Wham! literally any day of any year and I'll be happy. Christmas just makes people happy. The decorations are beautiful and the food is always delicious. I would die for Christmas to be celebrated for the longer. It's the happiest I am every year.

Besides, I'm in need of joy for finals this week. They've made me want to die. A few months ago I joked about dropping out of school because I'm broke, but maybe I'll drop out of school because I hate it and I might be stupid.

But it's fine. I just haven't slept in two ways.

All I have to do is make it to Friday at 4 o'clock. All of my finals will be done and I'll get to sleep. But first I'll get food. Food? No, maybe a milkshake. Shake up my normal order but oh, I should I order fries if I get a shake but I don't want fries I want mozzarella sticks but those don't go with milkshakes and I feel like someone's saying my name but I need to think about the milkshakes and mozzarella sticks because screw conventionalism, I'll order a milkshake and mozzarella sticks and-

"Evelyn," Michael interrupted my thoughts, his voice cutting through my internal spiral and his hand on my arm.

"I'm awake!" I shot up, suddenly realizing my head has started to fall.

"I don't think you were, sweetheart."

"No, no," I dismissed him. I was awake. Well, mostly awake. "You're wrong. I'm wide awake."

"Ev-"

"No Ev, I'm wide awake."

Michael sighed, "Do you remember when you told me I was gaslighting you that day at the beach?"

I nodded, too tired to connect the dots, but smiling at the fond memory.

"It seems we've come full circle in this relationship because now you're the one who's doing the gaslighting."

"If you're comparing me to Jake Gyllenhaal, this relationship over."

"Does that make me Taylor Swift? If so, I'm flattered."

"Ha!" I snacked his arm. "I knew you were listening to me this whole time."

"I always listen to you," Michael said fondly.

I learn forward to kiss him and he sighs, leaning into my touch. "Thank you," I whisper.

He nods and kisses me again mumbling, "you're welcome."

I hummed, "You should wear green more often, if looks good in you."

"You should sleep, you're wearing yourself out."

"I'll be fine," I say, opening my notes again. "I just need to study a little bit more so I can get this concept down before my final."

"Ev, you've said that the past two nights. You've studied so much, you're doing amazing. Give yourself a break."

"I will."

He gave me a skeptical look.

"I will," I insisted. "I just need to study until I'm sure I'll get a good grade."

"Okay. I'll stay here until you're done studying, then you have to go to sleep. Promise?"

"Promise."

~~~

For the second time in twenty four hours, I woke up to a gentle hand on my shoulder.

I didn't want to wake up. I was so, so comfy. The sun was hitting me and there was a warm blanket-

Wait.

Why is there a blanket on my shoulders? Why is the sun out? It's only 6 o'clock-

"What time is it?" I asked groggily.

"6 o'clock."

"Good," I sitting up a bit. "I wasn't asleep too long. I can still pull an all nighter."

"No, it's 6 in the morning."

Well, that woke me up.

"What? You're joking. Please tell me you're joking. I have class in 3 hours and-"

"And I'm going to bell you study. We have three hours and I watched some videos and looked over your notes last night and I think I came up with a way to help you study."

"Really? I have pages of notes, how did you get through it all?"

"Economics was ironically one of the only subjects I understood. And your notes were really thorough. Are you still nervous about the final?"

"You didn't have to do all that. You need to sleep too."

"That's hypocritical."

"Is it? I must've gotten that from my dad."
~~~

"You're funny. And deflecting."

"I learned that from my dad too," I smiled, eliciting no reaction from Michael. "Call me Jake Peralta because I'm on a roll with the dad jokes."

Michael deadpanned at me.

"Fine," I sighed. "I'm really nervous. What if all this studying has been for nothing? What if I fail?"

What if I fail?

One question and he knows my greatest fear.

"Ev, you're not going to fail. And even if you do, that's okay. Everyone's allowed to fail however many times they need to."

I couldn't stop the tear that slid down my cheek.

"Thank you, really." I cleared my throat, "no crying yet though. I need to study."

CPSIA information can be obtained
at www.ICGtesting.com
Printed in the USA
LVHW050812090123
736650LV00011BA/850

9 781837 617067